Sleeping Beauty, Indeed

Sleeping Beauty, Indeed

& Other Lesbian Fairytales

Edited by

JoSelle Vanderhooft

Lethe Press
Maple Shade, NJ

This paperback edition released 2009 by
Lethe Press, 118 Heritage Ave.
Maple Shade, NJ 08052

ISBN 1-59021-223-1 / 978-1-59021-223-3

An electronic edition of this anthology released in 2006 from Torquere Press.

Library of Congress Cataloging-in-Publication Data

Sleeping beauty, indeed & other lesbian fairytales / edited by JoSelle Vanderhooft.

p. cm.

Originally published: Round Rock, TX : Torquere Press, 2006.

ISBN 1-59021-223-1 (alk. paper)

1. Lesbians--Fiction. I. Vanderhooft, JoSelle. II. Title: Sleeping beauty, indeed and other lesbian fairytales.

PS648.L47S57 2009

813'.01083526643--dc22

2009028557

Sleeping Beauty, Indeed

Table of Contents

Introduction

JoSelle Vanderhooft

I've always been something of a sucker for fairytales of the retold variety. As a gawky child, and later as a gawky college student, I remember spending countless hours in my local libraries and bookstores devouring these things with the same ferocity many people devote only to chocolate. Yet, in all the contemporized fairytale books I shuffled home from the library, I noticed a conspicuous absence. Though feminist and multicultural renderings of old stories were well represented, I could have counted the number of lesbian-friendly retellings of old tales on less than one finger. As a gawky kid slowly coming to terms with her own non-straight sexuality, this silence was telling and somewhat deafening. What did these fairytale worlds with their attendant sleeping princess and handsome princes (who always seemed to end up married happily ever after) have to do with me? How did women who love women fit in alongside damsels in distress, fairy godmothers, magic and impossible tasks? Did we, indeed, have a place?

The tales comprising *Sleeping Beauty, Indeed* indicate that we not only have a place, but many places. Whether retelling old fairytales or creating new and exciting ones, these ten authors—some of them Torquere Press favorites—have created a collection of bold, romantic and frequently erotic stories of women who loved other women, once upon a time.

Fans of familiar stories such as "Cinderella" and Hans Christian Anderson's "The Little Mermaid" will find much to like in this collection. After a night of dancing with a careless prince named Charming, the heroines of these two stories meet on a beach in Meredith Schwarz's haunting and romantic "Undertow." Kimberly DeCina's "Voce"—about a forbidden and painful romance between an abused young woman and her wicked step-sister—is a heart-breaking retelling of the little-known Danish tale "Diamonds and Toads." For lighter fare, there's the anthology's titular story, Regan M. Wann's "Sleeping Beauty, Indeed"—a humorous take on the Charles Perrault tale as told from the point of view of one of the beleaguered fairy godmothers. Author Julia Talbot has also contributed "Coyote Kate of Camden" about the uproar caused in a little Colorado town by a tough-talking, female Pied Piper with a magic fiddle and an eye for virgins. For lovers of original fairytales, there's Erzebet YellowBoy's "Bird's-Eye View" about the romance between two princesses trapped in a tower and Frank M. Fradella's "The Seduction and Secret Life of Deirdre Fallon," an erotic tale of friendship between humans and fae in late Victorian England, among several others.

From the gently romantic to the profoundly erotic, the tales in *Sleeping Beauty, Indeed* are all stories I wish I could find at the nearest library. May they satisfy the gawky fairytale aficionado—and the reader who's always wanted Snow White and Rose Red to live happily ever after, together—in you.

JoSelle Vanderhooft
Lowell, Massachusetts
November, 2005

Two Sisters

R. Holsen

I

I wasn't but a girl when he came to the town, all shining hair like wheat in the fields and an easy smile. He'd the dirt on his face and dust on his pants of long travel, and the rickety old jalopy he'd drove up in didn't look as though it could have lasted. But when he took a room at Dora Mae's inn he said he'd come all the way from the Big River, and that was a three day's journey. Nothing for it but to believe him.

Dora Mae didn't believe him. She didn't like him much, either, at least that's what she said to anyone what would listen. Anne didn't like him but she did believe him, and Dora Mae said her disliking was only to cover that she couldn't stop staring. The third time she said that Anne stormed out of the inn and didn't come back for three days.

She weren't really our mother, either. At least, Dora Mae weren't my mother. But she'd been my mother's friend, like enough to a sister to her to when my mother died I got brought up at the inn floor with Anne, Will and the rest of the brood. Ricky didn't mind none, though he put up the old fight that it was just another mouth to feed. But when Anne and I got close and he brought me up to his knee, he told me a secret. That Dora Mae, when Mama had found out she weren't to have kids, had offered to have one for her. It'd been a miracle that I'd been born, though Mama took sick afterwards, and I always thought Dora Mae wished she'd gone and had me for Mama.

Things worked out all right. Dora Mae got me in the end, Mama got her baby girl though she didn't live long enough to meet me, not really. I weren't but a baby when she died. And Papa didn't stay long after that happened. He lit out like gangbusters and never looked back.

So it was me and Anne and Dora Mae and the family at the inn. And since the inn was where everything happened, and it wouldn't set to running if the people in town weren't nice to Dora Mae's family, I got brought up as family and no one said different.

They might have said somewhat if they knew about Anne and me, but they didn't. In all the years we lived there, I don't think anyone found out. Not till the day I left, nor maybe till the day I came back. But that's a whole different story.

II

Johnny was the most beautiful thing any girl in the town had ever seen. They were all walking about with painted faces and raised petticoats not two days after he set up shop in the hardware store with the boys. He'd cleaned up good by then, sharp brown suit and taken a razor to his face. One daring girl who I don't remember anymore, though I can remember the look on her face plain as day when she said it, told everyone who'd listen that his skin was soft as rabbit fur. I didn't know from rabbit fur then, but it seemed pretty fine to me.

He was nice enough, well-spoken and well-looking. He'd tip his cap to every lady and walk one across the street if it was late, but he never paid anyone especial attention. At least, not that I saw.

Not that they didn't try. And not that their mothers didn't try, and even their fathers when they saw he weren't going to be no lay about or rake like some of the others what came into town that summer. Everyone tried to get a piece of poor Johnny that year. He was new, special and sweet like that whole summer. I laughed when I thought about how chased the poor boy was. Last year it had been Heather's boy, Patrick. This year it was the pretty piece, Johnny. Next year it'd be some other mother's son, but he didn't know that yet.

I think it upset him more than most, 'cause of the not knowing. He covered it pretty good, though. The only ones he'd even talk to about it were me and Will, 'cause of working at the inn and him making all the deliveries. He'd sneak in the back and ask one or the other of us if there was anyone laying about in wait for him, and thank us when we snuck him back out again.

"It weren't nothing," I told him once. "And it's nothing to anyone whether you find a girl or not, or marry at all, or leave with the snow next spring. It's just that you're new, and they all chase after the new boy."

He didn't seem to like that, which I thought was pretty funny of him. But he kissed my cheek and thanked me for the telling and went back to the store. I'd had a couple boys try that, but he was the first one I didn't mind it from. Maybe 'cause I knew he didn't mean it.

Anne thought he did, though. She asked me about it that same night as we were making ready for bed, and the whole week after. What did I think I was doing with that boy, she asked, and did I plan on walking out with him. I just figured she were jealous or something like, kept telling her and holding her even with her being five years older. She was always so scared that I'd leave, anyway. After a while she stopped asking, and I figured on her coming to realize that Johnny weren't nothing but a pretty friend anyway.

A good friend, too. That autumn he came by more often, settling down as the girls started to drop away one by one. They were finally seeing that he'd no interest in any of them, which was nice for him and better for the other boys. Especially Hugh, who'd been stomping around the inn all muttering and dark-like over Alice taking to her bed 'cause Johnny wouldn't walk with her. It'd been a crazy summer when he came puttering into town, and I'd thought it was all finally starting to come back to regular.

Will and Johnny made friends. Will'd been all quiet and in the corners playing with his knife and some piece of wood or another, and Johnny had taken to bringing him scraps to carve on. At first Will made me talk to him, which I thought was all silly and more like the girls with their paint and hose, but after a while he said it was only 'cause he didn't want to seem stupid in front of the older boy. So that was all right. And after a while Johnny started talking to him by his own self anyway, and they got to talking about fishing and whittling and other things I'd no interest in.

Hugh didn't like Johnny much, said he'd been sniffing around me all summer, but I told him he was full of horse-stuff and where he could put his funny ideas. Anne heard us, of course, and she didn't like it either. But she didn't talk to Hugh much anymore, not since Hugh'd started to look at her funny for keeping me in her room past when I should have left.

"Never mind Hugh," I told her. "He don't understand a lot of things about the way the world's tail wags, has to walk outside to see that it's raining. He's got a good heart and he loves you, being his sister and all, he just don't understand it."

She didn't much like that. "If that's his way of being a brother, he can take his love and ..."

We had a fight about that, too, but since no one did anything nor tried to stop us, there weren't much that came of it.

Come winter and Christmas-time, Johnny was fair to being part of the family. Even Dora Mae decided he'd do, at least to come have dinner with us since he didn't have no family in the town. He'd a mother and little brother, he said, but they were far off and he was waiting till he'd enough money to put them both up before sending for them. Which was all right and fair, as far as that went. Weren't the first time a young man'd wandered off to seek his fortune, though it'd been a long time since the town was greener pastures for someone.

He'd brought a few presents for each of us, but none so fine as the beaver-fur cap he gave me. I thought it were a joke at first, or some kind of apology, only I couldn't think of what he'd done or said that he would be apologizing for. Or maybe it was something he'd want a favor for in exchange, but he didn't ask for nothing after that. Will gave me a funny look and a smile, like he knew what it was all about. I didn't understand, not then anyway.

Dora Mae did, and she had words with him afterwards out by the barn. Had words loud enough that we could hear their voices in our room, though I couldn't make out all the words. My name was in there, and Anne's, and Will's. Didn't know who else she spoke about, though.

Anne didn't talk to me for a week after that. Jealous again, I figured. She didn't like none of the boys paying attention to me, but that was all right, since I weren't interested in them anyway. Johnny was sweet and all, but he weren't special enough to make me sit up and take notice. But nothing I'd say to her would make her listen, so I just had to wait that long and awful week until she'd done with her snit. The last day that beaver-skin cap went missing, but I didn't mind too much.

Not that it weren't a fine thing, and one I'd liked showing off just to see the looks on those girls' faces. But it wasn't a cold winter, and I'd no need of it anyway. Plus, Anne was worth twenty beaver-skin caps, and if the disappearance of one were all it took to get her talking to me again, that was well worth it and all.

III

Winter came and went and sure as spring thaw the girls found another boy to squeal over. This year it was Lenny with his eyes blue as cornsilk flowers, and Johnny had a bit of a rest. One or two still pursued him as a likely prospect, or rather their mothers did, but this time it was more on account of his growing prosperity and the idea that he might make some poor girl a decent husband. Couldn't fault the mothers for that, I guess, specially seeing as how the girls themselves were sweet folk but a little on the wild side, and might be needing a husband soon to explain away the extra mouth.

Johnny still came over to Dora Mae's, though, bringing his wood and his nails and whatever else we might be needing, or whatever else he and Will got up to. As the weather turned more pleasant he started bringing over his fishing pole and took to trying to get me and Anne out to the lake, but Anne wouldn't have none of it. She still didn't like him, I saw, and wouldn't associate longer than she had to or Dora Mae told her to. I still didn't understand none of that, but it was easier not to argue about it, nor to bring it up to her unless she was in a fine mood.

Then, later, it was Hugh and Mary's wedding that did it. Everyone turned out for the ceremony, all delighted and such and wishing them all kinds of well. Johnny had taught Will to dance beforehand, and it turned out that a lot of the girls decided that night they liked the look of my baby brother.

Of course, a couple of them liked the look of Johnny, still, as well, especially with his hair all slick back and his clothes all new and pressed and clear of sawdust. He didn't want to talk to none of them though, didn't seem to want to talk to any girls at all.

So you can bet I was surprised when he caught me sneaking out of the party, said he wanted to talk to me. Said he'd got Dora Mae's permission and everything, and I just stared at him 'cause I had no idea what he meant.

"With your brother all married and suchlike, and you all grown—" I'd had my sixteenth earlier that winter, you see, not that it meant much in the town except that I'd get to keep what money I earned working at the inn. Dora

Mae was strict about that. "—she said it would be okay. If you wanted to, that is."

I still didn't understand. "Wanted to? Say what you mean, Johnny, my mind weren't up to reading yours even before the wedding."

"It's early and all," he was smiling, though, like he expected things to have a happy ending. I still was wandering somewhere around the middle, not knowing what he wanted to come out. "And I wouldn't expect nothing before at least a year, maybe longer. But." He didn't say nothing further, just pulled a gold ring from out his pocket and showed it to me like it was supposed to mean something.

I guess it was, though for a minute or two I didn't know for the life of me what was going on. And then I put it together, like it was too strange for my mind to figure as being real and I had to think about it a moment.

"Johnny, what on God's green earth do you mean by this?"

He got all sad at that, and I guessed he hadn't expected me to come over all surprised. And maybe it came out a little meaner than I'd meant it to.

"I mean, you're nice and all, and I like you like a brother. But, Johnny, whatever did I do to make you think I wanted…"

"I thought you knew." He really was all sad, and hurting something fiercer than I'd ever seen him before. "I thought … well, it doesn't matter, I suppose." His voice had that bird-warble kind of note to it, like he was trying not to cry. And boys didn't cry, not really, though I'd seen Will not-crying half a dozen times behind the barn. I thought this might be like one of those times, but Johnny only shook his head.

"I'm sorry ..." I didn't know what else to say, if anything else could make it better. Maybe all his hopes, all his dreams of a house of his own and a family he could show his Ma had been resting on me. I hoped not; I'd never been interested in boys, and all Johnny's sweet manners and pretty looks couldn't make up for that. But I guess he hadn't figured that part out yet.

"It's all right." He smiled at me anyway, putting on a brave front. "Keep it, anyhow. For luck."

I figured as how he just didn't want to have it sitting around to remind him. I wouldn't have, if I'd been him. But Anne didn't see it that way, though she didn't yell like I expected her to. She just looked at it, and was quiet for a long time, and then when she looked up at me again she was crying.

"I didn't say yes," I tried to tell her. She was sad anyhow, maybe sad that I'd let Johnny go on believing, though I wouldn't have understood why. It wasn't as though she'd liked him. Or maybe she was just sad that someone had thought of it first, though there weren't no pastor in the country who'd marry us, anyhow. "I didn't say yes, Annie."

"Then what's this?" And she picked up the ring and chucked it at my head. I ducked, of course, you don't work in an inn all your life and not learn to duck when people chuck things at your head. But part of me was screeching like the miller's wife in the back of my head, wondering what she was talking about. "That's not exactly a no, innit?

"It's not a yes, Annie." It didn't look like a no, to be truthful, but it wasn't as though I was out celebrating a yes with Johnny. Not the way he'd skulked off back to the hardware store to mourn his loss alone or with a bottle.

And I knew she'd seen him do it, because she'd seen us part ways after the conversation. And then she'd stalked up to our room at the inn.

"But you didn't exactly put him off, did you?" she yelped, and I just knew half the guests could hear her. "All that summer and winter he was coming sniffing around like a dog in heat and …"

"And nothing!" This time it was just her being stupid, and I don't know why but I felt like telling her that. "Annie, he was coming around here 'cause of Will! To go fishing and whittling and whatever all boys do, not for me, for Will. I wasn't expecting that damn thing any more than you were when he popped up all smiles and asking."

"Wasn't like no one else could have told you," she snapped. That hurt, though it did remind me that he'd said he'd talked to Dora Mae about it.

"Your Momma might could have told me, but that's only 'cause he asked her first. And she probably told him I weren't having none of him." Anne's Momma had never talked to us about it, but she knew. I knew she knew, could see it in her eyes when she looked at us. She didn't seem to mind none, either, which was a blessing.

"Then why'd he go and have to ask you like that?"

I shook my head, couldn't explain none of it. And I sat down on the bed and tried to think of how, but there weren't no good explanation coming to mind. "I don't know, Annie, I really don't. Johnny's a sweet boy, but he's just a little messed up in the head. Thinking a smile means a yes and there ain't a cloud in the sky when it's near halfway to flooding. He'll find some other girl and forget all about tonight, soon enough."

I didn't think Anne thought any more about it after that night, after we made up and all. I didn't think it bothered her, except that Johnny's come sniffing around and asking after me.

IV

I thought it were all over the next day when we went walking down by the Little Snake. She seemed happier, anyhow, a little more smiling and the day was nice. We'd gotten the day off work and packed a lunch and a blanket, figured on not being back till evening. At least, that's what I figured.

She held my hand as we walked, Anne with her light step and her skirt all whirling in the breeze. She'd an easier time of it that day than she'd had in months. Smiling more often and the like, and she held me and kissed me like she hadn't in a long time. I didn't put it together then, all the times and all the days lining up like ripples after a skipped stone. All I knew was that we were happy, and the day was good.

And then we went wading in the river, and the cold water like to have frozen my toes solid. I got in halfway and stopped, my skirts all bunched up and lifted in my hands so as not to get much more than the lace at the edges wet.

I thought I'd tripped and fallen when I saw the river rising up. It didn't quite fit, the way my face was in the water and wouldn't come up, not with the hands on my back and neck. My skin went cold and numb and my chest started to burn. It all went black, though I could still hear the birds singing and the water rising up above my body.

"You shouldn'ta taken him, Molly," she told me in that tearful, choked up voice. "You shouldn'ta done that."

It was dark for a long time. She picked up my skirts and I guessed they'd been caught on a rock or somewhat, 'cause the water started pushing me down-stream and over the falls. My eyes weren't coming back, but I could still hear like it was coming down a long canyon, everything distant and strange.

Day and night didn't make no difference with my eyes closed as they were, or whatever was causing the blackness. The next thing I knew was different was hands on my shoulders, on my dress, pulling me up and out of the water. I could barely tell what they were, boy's hands or man's, with the cold making my skin all numb-like. It was the creaking of the mill-wheel that did it, I recognized that from the town. Didn't hear none of the town's other noises, though. Must have been a mill down the river.

He was talking to some other man, the miller was. My ears still weren't working right, I couldn't hear what they were saying, but the tone of their words suggested they were bargaining over something. It sounded like a market, or a deal at a market, never mind that there weren't no sounds of anything what might have been being bartered over. I guess it must have been my own self, because the next thing I knew they'd thrown me into a wagon. I still couldn't move. Funny, too, that I wasn't scared over it. Just waiting there for something to happen, though I couldn't have said what it might be.

The cart took me a-ways, couldn't have said how far or how long. But the next thing I knew I was being tugged at again, laid out on what might have been a bench or a table. It was hard wood under my soon-to-be-naked back, and then water through my hair and over my face, over my body.

That's when the pain begun, of course. I'd just started to feel all right about what strangeness was happening when he started tugging at my hair, so hard that it fell out in his hands. And then he took a knife to me, and I still weren't afraid, though he must have been gutting me like a fish. There were all those wet sounds like I used to hear at the butchers when I went over to collect the day's meat, sounds of someone messing about when someone's insides were on their outside.

After that things started to go a little funny. It seems to me I must have been gone asleep for a long time. When I next started to hear things it was different, like. Sharper and sounded almost like music, and there was a shiver going all through my body. A man was singing, and it seemed as I wanted to sing along with him. So I did.

He stopped. I guess he hadn't reckoned on that, and he moved around fair as to spill me off his lap. Funny, I hadn't realized I was on his lap until that moment.

"Who's there?"

I wanted to speak out, couldn't. I didn't know why either, but I still weren't scared. It occurred to me that I should have been, but I weren't. I just looked at him without my eyes, listened to the sound of his voice.

"Who's there?"

I couldn't make no sound, but when he touched me again to pick me up I could sing, and I did. Told him my name and my whole story, and he listened all silent-like as though it were the most shocking thing he'd heard in his life. Maybe it was. Or maybe he just weren't used to things like I was then talking. I wasn't sure what I was then, either girl or corpse or ghostly spirit. I weren't alive, I'd figured that much out by then.

V

He took me back home, to my town, in the end. It turned out as he was a minstrel of the traveling sort, parted ways from his company for a little while as he visited folks he'd had in the nearby. And he was set to go on the road again and rejoin, but I persuaded him otherwise.

As we came closer the voices turned familiar, and I could hear the chink and rattle and stamp of every horse. It all turned into a song that reminded me of home, though in a way I'd never thought of before. I was still seeing things in that new way, if you could really call it seeing. Didn't hear anyone call for me though, nor hear anyone gasp or stare. Whatever way I looked to others, it must not have been such as anyone would recognize me from it.

We went into Dora Mae's, I could tell it just that instant from the sounds. Will's voice was still there, Hugh and Mary must have been over for that night. Lenny's voice was all mixed up with some girl's I didn't recognize, sounding like she might possibly have been his wife by the things they said. I wasn't sure how long I'd been gone and changed.

The man who'd had me and taken care of me went up to Dora Mae and said something I couldn't make out. Then I felt him lift me up, showing me to her I think. She gasped and her hand smacked on the counter-top, making a pretty ring-thud.

Next thing I knew there was a shout, then more people shouting. Dora Mae was running about the inn, banging on doors and rousing everyone. Last time I'd heard her do that there'd been a fire at the hostelry, but that was three years gone now. I'd no idea what was going on this time.

Couldn't see anything, and couldn't hear proper. My skin, if I had any left, was all numb. Couldn't smell if there was smoke or taste it on my tongue, if I still had that as well. Weren't no way for me to tell what was going on, but the minstrel's hand stayed on my shoulder and kept me where I was.

Next thing I knew I was hearing Anne's voice, sounding all scared and worried. Anne, my sweet little Annie, littler but older than me and all grown up and scared now.

And there was Johnny's voice, and Will was right by my ear asking in ways that sounded like he was about to cry, or scream, or something else un-manly like. I wanted to ask what was going on, and couldn't.

Dora Mae's hand was on my shoulder next. At least I guessed it was her, 'cause of her voice being right above me. She was calm, as calm now as she'd been terrified earlier, or busy. The whole room went quiet, like they were waiting for someone to speak out and explain what was happening. There were more shuffling feet in that common room than I'd ever heard in all my years of living at the inn.

"Go on," he said, the minstrel man. "Tell them what happened."

There were a couple gasps, a couple people murmuring like he'd gone crazy. But his hands started to move and I couldn't help it, I spoke up like I'd never been silenced.

I told them everything. About Johnny, about what he'd given me and what he'd asked me. I told them how sweet he'd been to Will and how he'd always been hanging about the place, though it wasn't as no one could have seen or remembered that. There were a couple of noises when I started speaking, someone coughing and someone sobbing, but I couldn't tell who.

I told them about me and Anne.

Johnny gasped at that. Poor pretty Johnny, I remembered the sound of his voice. And someone near him started to shuffle but I couldn't tell who it was, so I just kept talking. And I told them about how, the day after Johnny'd made his proposal all innocent-like and then sad that he'd mistook me, how Anne had pushed me in the river and drowned me like an unwanted puppy.

There was a thud right by where I'd heard Johnny's gasp before. Must have been Anne, I guessed, standing right by him.

And it wasn't me she'd been jealous of then, but Johnny. It wasn't me she'd cried and screamed over, it'd been pretty Johnny with his golden hair. I should have been upset with her, with him. I should have yelled and screamed and done to her as she'd done to me, but I couldn't even if I'd wanted to and whatever strange state I was in now, I didn't want to anymore. I was just there, still, and if I was anything I was only tired and maybe just a little bit sad.

"Anne." I could speak, if I couldn't do anything else. "My sweet Anne. Why'd you go and do it, honey? Why?"

She didn't say a word. I heard her footsteps tearing on out of there like she was on fire, and then a crash. Then a splash, and silence. Someone yelled as how she'd tipped over and fallen down the well. Drowned herself, as she'd drowned me. I just sighed. It made sense, anyway.

I didn't speak again.

Bones Like Black Sugar

Catherynne M. Valente

Why did I ever go back? Isn't it enough that the eggs fry evenly in my iron pan, that the white edges crisp so prettily, like doilies, that the chimney huffs its smoke grandfather-satisfied, that the green trees stay in their civilized trim, that they will never again reach out for me as they did in those days, brackish arms a-bramble? Isn't it enough to serve a brute-blond brother in my smooth apron, to bow a braided head before him as before a husband, and make sure his coffee had enough chicory, enough milk? I have a house of my own, of wood and stone, with violets eating earth in the shadow of an iron-hinged door, and not a sparkle of sugar in any cupboard, on any tongue.

He told me it would be enough. With a brown hand he took up the axe in the woodpile, and built a house around me, up, up, up, a house with no windows, where I could crack my eggs like knuckles, and polish stairs until my fingers wore away. He forbade me to boil chocolate in a silver tin; he forbade me to stretch taffy between my fingers for the village children; he forbade me to comb honey from any hive. There was milk enough, and bread enough, and meat slung across the table, glistening with fat.

And still I go back. To her, to the glen, to the ruins of her house casting shadows like spice on the grass.

Over and over, the moon slashes windows into the black soil while he sleeps behind me, sleeps dead and sweat-pooled. My steps grin on the pine needles and I need no breadcrumbs, never needed breadcrumbs, north into the forest, the wood, the thicket of breath and branches that pricks my skull hours on hours, that tangles my lungs in sap and sweet. It is not that I remember where it is, but my feet have learned no other path than this, this crow-hung track slinking through the dark. They turn and point with the eagerness of a girl in pigtails, a girl in braids, a girl with ribbons streaming like oaths behind her.

Between two midnights it appears, no warning, a waft of silver and sallow, blades bent over like broken flutes, a disc of grasslight whispering to itself. The ruins are classical, Athenian: charred banisters of twisted licorice and cherry-sticky stairs leading up to the star-bowels, crumble-barren. The butterscotch-and-toffee floor is half-eaten by mice and voles, its shards flashing cloud-quick—on its scalded surface, bubbles long hardened into checkered barrows, stood shattered furniture: praline fauteuils roasted into stumps, marzipan sideboards shot through with burst sugar-glass and icing-china, a molten headboard twisted into a shimmer of jellybean slag, linen-ashes of peppermint and raspberry seeds, still floating windwise after all this time. The smell is still thick as scarves: burnt candy, everywhere, the carbuncle-heart of sugar seething in its endless boil, vanished jam-mortar and confection-white rainspouts, crystalline panes crusted with sweet, peanut brittle rafters and gingerbread walls, all wheeling in their invisible cotillion, gobbling the air into syrup.

And there is the oven.

It is a good German oven, squat as a heart, whole and leering. Its cacao-grille gapes throat-open, and I want it to be full of ashes this time, I want it to be purified, scrubbed empty and clean as an oven ought to be. I know each time I breathe the air of that furnace that I will always taste of this house, I will taste of witch and grief, I will taste of the laughing fire even as I taste of wife and sister. The smell of flesh cooking will cling to my nose, the cloy of gold teeth melting will stick in my sleeves.

I will never recover from this, I will never be well, I will never grow up.

It ought to be scoured of meat and grease and burst irises—but she slumps out of it, stuck, now as all the other times, her candied pelvis caught on the broiling pan, fleshless arms stretched out in supplication, frozen in the grace of a ruined arch, the skeleton of an angel consumed, angles all wrong, ribs descending black as treble scales, femurs like cathedral columns dripping with honey-gold. Her eyes stare into the loam, gape-hollow. Her teeth have broken on the root of a snarling yew—they scatter on the wet grass like Easter eggs. Her skull has burst open where it struck a stone. There a jagged rupture where her fontanel must have been—when she was an infant, when she was pure, when her eyes were large and bright as peppermint wheels and she had a mother, somewhere far off and unimaginable, where women like her are made.

Every time is the same.

I gather her up into my arms, tenderly, bone by bone. I have to be careful—she falls apart so easily; her desiccated ligaments surrender without struggle. It would be poetic to carry her up the stairs, a dead bride, but there is no need, and the stairs lead to nothing but windburnt night. Instead, I bear her to the decrepit bed, its vanilla coverlet curled back like the pages of a spoiled book, the pillows cinnamon-cinders. The harlequin relic that was once a high-postered frame casts shadows of berry and blue, pools of emerald like gumdrops on the sheets. I lay her down like a princess, arrange her bones like runes, never forgetting to keep her head balanced in my hand, infant-gently, as I pull her sternum into place, her clavicle, her jaw, her delicate wrists crossing over my shoulders.

And I put my face to her scorched cheek; I fold my body into hers, into the light of the candy-ruins.

And I hold her to me, like the child I was, the chubby girl with lacy skirts peering out of her cage.

And I breathe: her bones move with my breath. My pulse swims: hers rustles like a wood in winter.

And under my arms there is flesh, there is a taste like cakes in a pretty window, there is a rush of hair darker than ovens. Under my lips there are lips like floss, and my eyelashes beat against warm skin, beading with caramel-sweat.

She smiles at me, she smiles at me and the belly under my hands is Turkish delight, she smiles as if I had never pushed her, as if I had come to her house alone and stood student-bright at the stove while she baked her new bookshelves, as if there was no smoke or flame. She smiles like erasure, she smiles like a confessor. She swells with candy like a mother, her green eyes opening and closing, and under my hands she is beautiful, beautiful, under my hands she is innocent, I am innocent, there is nothing which is not white, which is not a scald of purity, which does not flare with light.

And she forgives me, she forgives me, her heavy arms draped over me like curtains, her demoniac mouth red and bloody at my ear. I hold out my breasts to her like an apology and I beg, I beg her to make me like her, make of my body a window or a cellar door, peach-sweet and clear as glass, grind my bones to sugar, braid my hair into bell-pulls of saltwater taffy and punish me, punish me, I ought to be punished, I ought to be burned, I ought to have gone into the oven with you, into the fire, into the red and the ash, and my blood ought to have boiled over your hands, and my marrow ought to have smelted into yours, and my skull ought to shatter on the stone where my fontanel must have been, and the shards of it, the shards of it ought to have mingled with yours when the leaves fell, ought to have been indistinguishable, ought to have, ought to have! Devour me now as you promised, swallow me, I am offering it, carve me into light and dark and I will be your obedient supper—don't leave me, don't look at him, don't chose him, he does not love you, and he will taste of bracken and snails—take me up into your iron pot and I will boil for you, if you ask it, if you will stay with me and all the while call me sweet, call me sweet. You promised, my love, you promised to destroy me.

Under my hands you are so young. Under my hands you laugh like blackbirds' wings.

And I put my hands to her in the sweetshop-graveyard of her house.

And I hold her to me like a widow—she is wet with my weeping, my tears a melt of plums.

And I breathe: there is no answer. My pulse pleads: there is no echo.

And under my arms there is nothing, nothing but her bones like black sugar, and the chasm of her dead mouth yawning at the moon.

The Mute Princess

AJ Grant

(Based on the Yemeni fairy tale of the same name.)

It came to pass that there was a kingdom with a king and queen who had but one child: a daughter whom they loved with all the devotion that they could have shown to a thousand children, or even to a son.

The princess was gifted with hair as black as raven's wings, eyes as dark as the shadows of the moon, lips like rubies from the deepest jungle, and hands as small and delicate as the wings of a butterfly. She was the most beautiful maiden in all the kingdom, and all who saw her wished to have her for their own.

However it was not her beauty which made the princess known throughout the land; it was her silence. Ever since the occasion of her birth the princess spoke not one single word. Neither her father nor mother nor any who came to call upon her could get her to talk.

There were many who believed the princess was born mute, and that not even the highest magicks could break her silent spell. But the king and queen believed differently. They knew in their hearts that their beloved child could talk but that she would not do so until inspired to by the right reason.

During this time there were lords, princes and even kings who came calling upon the castle. Each of them begged for the right to court the princess, and to make her their bride. Though the king despaired at the thought of his daughter finding no love or companionship of her own, he sent all of her would-be suitors away, believing that there was no way to discover if any of them were truly worthy of the princess, or even if she cared for them.

Then one day his wife, the queen, made a suggestion. "Let us make a test," she said. "Let her decide for herself who she wishes. If there is one that she wants, surely she will break her silence. If she remains mute, they do not deserve her company."

And so the king issued a proclamation: Those who wished to wed the princess were permitted to spend one night with her in the presence of a witness. Any who could get the princess to speak even as much as one single word could take the princess for their bride. Any who failed would be hanged on the gallows at dawn.

In another kingdom that was far, far away was a princess by the name of Adira. Adira was both beautiful and wise. She loved to spend her days reading in the great library of her mother's castle, and speaking with the sages and old women who advised her mother and who knew the secrets of the earth and the hidden languages of the stars.

So dedicated to learning was she that one day she appeared before her mother the empress and made a request.

"I wish to travel," Adira said. "I wish to go beyond the mountains of our land and speak to all whom I meet and learn from any who would teach me. Only then shall I be learned and wise enough to rule once you have gone."

The empress felt that this was a sensible thing for her daughter to do, but worried about the dangers that such a journey could present. She took seven days and seven nights to make her decision. She consulted with her advisors, and prayed for guidance.

On the eighth day she spoke to her daughter.

"Go forth," the empress said, "for I have asked the wizards and wise women, I have read the moon and planets, and spoken to the tortoise who knows where the phoenix keeps its egg. They have told me that you will learn much on your travels, and that this will make you a great ruler. They have also told me that you will find your destiny. But, my child, be safe! For your destiny will charge you with a dangerous task, and if you do not succeed by the end one year and one day then I shall never see you again."

Adira took the empress's words into her heart and set out the next day to begin her journey. She traveled far and wide. She visited the valley where the sun hid inside of caves made of diamonds. She met the old man who knew how to make cloth that could trap mice and turn them into carpenters. She saw the town where the river's water was made of honey, and the village where all babies were born with the gift of song.

She learned much on her journey, and performed many tasks. But no task felt like the task of her destiny.

Adira kept traveling, keeping her eye watchful upon the cycle of the moon, knowing that she dared not remain in one place too long lest her time run out, and she never would see her mother or homeland again.

It was thus, on the first night of the last full moon before Adira failed in her destiny, that she came into the land of the mute princess and heard of the king's proclamation.

"Go to the king," Adira said to her most trusted handmaiden. "Give him this chest of gold and the flute which plays King Solomon's lullaby. Tell him that I wish to meet his princess."

The handmaiden did as she was told. She returned quickly with an invitation for Adira to come before the throne. Adira dressed herself in her finest garments and presented herself to the king and queen in their great hall.

"My proclamation was for any who wished to make my daughter their bride," the king said.

"I know, sir," Adira replied.

"You are not a prince," the king said, his eyes like beetles as they gazed upon her. "Nor are you a king."

"I am myself, sir," Adira said, keeping her hands folded in front of her. "I can but hope the princess will find some worth in me."

"It does no harm to let her try," the queen said.

"Do you understand my challenge?" the king asked.

Adira faced the king bravely, but humbly. "I do, sir. I understand that the prize for winning is your daughter. I understand that the prize for failure is death."

"You accept the challenge with both outcomes before you?" the king asked.

"I do, sir," Adira said. "For I have been told I would embrace my destiny before the moon now above us grows dark again."

The king accepted Adira's request. He allowed her into the chambers of the princess, leaving them alone save for one witness who would tell the king if the princess spoke or not.

Upon seeing the princess, Adira knew that she had met her destiny, for the princess was fairer than the finest silks or jewels and the light of her smile made Adira's heart grow as large as the eye of an elephant. Adira knew that she would accept the gallows gladly if she could not prove herself worthy.

Adira set her mind to the challenge of getting the princess to speak. Hours passed, with only the sound of the princess' needlework to keep them company. Finally Adira turned to the witness and spoke.

"Let us have a conversation, you and I," Adira said. "Let us learn from one another, for I wish to know many things before I die and tomorrow morning I shall be hanged."

"It is not for me to speak," the witness replied, folding her arms across her ample bosom. "My job is to listen."

"If I gave you a question, could you reply?" Adira asked.

"It may be possible," the witness admitted.

"Excellent," Adira said, "for there is a puzzle that vexes me. I was once told a story of a nobleman, his wife, and their servant. They took to walking one day and ended up in a field far from all who knew them. A band of robbers came upon them, made greedy by the sight of the nobleman's fine clothing and the sound of the money in his pockets.

The robbers attacked, beheading the nobleman and his servant and stealing all of their gold.

"The nobleman's wife fell to the ground in despair. She beat her breast, rent her garments, and wept bitter tears as the sun set and the day became night.

"Then, in the darkness, she heard voices. Two owls had heard her cry. They sat in the tree above her, talking about her tragedy. 'How sad!' said one of the owls 'For this is a gentle woman who is pious and charitable and turns no beggar away from her castle. What shame that there is no way anyone can help her.'

"'But there is,' said the second owl. 'Did you not know that this tree is a tree of life? She could anoint their bodies with the juice of the fruit that grows here and place the men's heads upon their necks. When the sun rises it will chase away the darkness and death, and she will be with her beloved husband and faithful servant once more.'

"The noblewoman was very grateful for this knowledge. She sprang to her feet, took the juice of the fruit, and anointed the bodies of the two men as the owls had instructed. She placed the heads upon the necks and then waited for the dawn.

"When the dawn came the men did rise, but the noblewoman saw that she had made a terrible mistake. With no light to guide her she had placed her husband's head on the body of their servant, and their servant's head on the body of her husband. There was no way to undo what she had done.

"The two men began to argue over the woman, each claiming that she was their wife. The woman was loyal to her husband, but did not know if she was now married to the husband's head on the servant's body, or the husband's body beneath the servant's head. I know of this tale," Adira said, "but I do not know the solution. To whom does the woman belong?"

"That is a vexing question," the witness agreed. "We must wait until morning and ask the wisest in the kingdom."

"But I cannot," Adira said. "Come dawn I will be hanged. I will die not knowing the answer."

It was then that the princess, who had listened to the tale with as much interest as the witness, found she could not keep silent in the light of such a meaningful question. "She belongs to the husband's head on the servant's body," the princess said. "For it is the head which holds all wisdom and the memory of the many years of his love for his wife. The body is but a shell, no different from any other once clothes are placed upon it."

The witness was very startled to hear words from the princess. But Adira smiled, taking care to bow her head politely as she said, "Thank you, your highness. You are indeed very wise and learned in such matters. I am certain that you are right. It is important to remember that wisdom and memory of a lifetime of love do not depend upon the body. I thank you for your counsel."

The next morning the witness told the king and queen what had happened. The king was filled with disbelief at the thought of anyone having finally proven worthy of hearing his daughter's voice, and accused the witness of lying to him. He readied to summon the executioner, but the queen stopped him before he could place the command.

"It is a fair witness," the queen said, "and trustworthy. If you have doubt, give the test again. Have Adira spend a second night with our daughter and choose another witness to aid in keeping watchful eye upon them. If our daughter does not speak, you can execute Adira come morning."

The king agreed that this was a fair compromise. So it came to pass that on the second night of the last full moon of the time of Adira's destiny that she was sent back to the princess' chambers, this time with two witnesses to stand watch over them.

It seemed to Adira that the princess smiled when she appeared, but the smile was as fleeting as a tadpole in a stream, and the princess once more bent to her needlework and sat in silence.

Adira watched her, marveling at the skill with which the princess handled the thread, her touch as swift and clever as a spider's with its silk. Adira knew with more surety than ever that she and the princess were meant to be together, if only Adira could prove worthy of her.

As had happened the night before, hours passed with no words spoken by anyone. Finally Adira turned to the two witnesses. "Let us speak, and learn from one another. For I wish to learn many things before I die and tomorrow I shall be hanged."

"We do not speak," the second witness told her. "Our job is to listen."

"Can you answer a question if I ask one of you?" Adira asked.

"It is possible," the first witness admitted.

"Excellent," Adira said, "for I have a puzzle which vexes me. I have heard a tale of three women who traveled together. One had a mirror that could see to the far corners of the world. Another had a carpet which could fly any distance in the time it took to take a step. The third had a potion that could cure any illness, even that of death.

"One day the woman with the mirror looked into it and saw a funeral procession with mourners who filled the streets of an enormous town, each one crying and following behind a coffin inlaid with jewels and gold and silver.

"The woman told her companions what she saw. The one with the flying carpet unrolled it at once, bidding her friends to get on it. 'We shall go to the funeral and honor whoever has died, for surely it must be an important and noble person.'

"The three women sat upon the carpet and in the time it took to take a step they were at the funeral. They asked of those around them, 'Who is it? Who was it that died?' They were told that it was the king's daughter, who was wise and beautiful and kind to all in the kingdom. She had been cursed by a jealous fox, who had envied her cunning and beauty.

"Upon hearing of this injustice the three women went before the king, telling him that they could cure his daughter. The king was so grateful he fell to his knees before them, promising his kingdom to the one who could return his daughter to life again.

"The third woman went to the chamber where the princess' body was kept. Knowing the dead could not swallow, the woman took some of the potion into her own mouth. She placed her lips over that of the princess' and kissed her, dancing her tongue over lips and teeth until enough of the potion had dribbled inside for the princess' cheeks to flush, her mouth to open, her lungs to gasp and the rest of the potion be swallowed.

"Upon seeing his daughter restored the king cried out with great joy, and reminded the three women of his promise to grant his kingdom to the one who had cured her.

"The three women began to argue, each pointing out that they had had a hand in the task and therefore deserved to be given the kingdom. I know of this tale," Adira said, "but I do not know the solution. To whom does the kingdom belong?"

"That is a vexing question," the second witness agreed. "We must wait until morning and ask the counsel of the wisest in the kingdom."

"But I cannot," Adira said. "Come dawn I will be hanged. I will die not knowing the answer."

And then the princess, who had put her needlework down so that she might stare at Adira and give her full attention to the story, said, "It is the third woman who has earned the kingdom. The first saw the princess and the second brought them swiftly, but without the potion of the third woman the princess' heart would not have quickened and returned her to life. It is she who completed the task."

"Thank you, your highness," Adira said, bowing respectfully. "You are very learned and wise. I am certain you are correct. It is important to remember who has made the princess' heart beat quickly. Thank you for your counsel."

Come morning, the two witnesses appeared before the king and queen. The two witnesses told the story of what had happened. Again the king was disbelieving that his daughter had spoken, again the queen advised him to give Adira the benefit of the doubt.

So it came to pass that Adira was sent back to the princess' chambers on the third night of the last full moon exactly one year and one day from the time Adira had left her mother and her homeland. This time there were three witnesses, and Adira knew that if she failed she would be hanged, and her mother would never see her again.

On this night the princess had no needlework. She sat in waiting, dressed in a garment of as rich and deep a red as her lips with her dark hair unbound and fallen like lace about her pale white shoulders. Her eyes met Adira's as she entered the room, but as before the princess remained silent.

Adira did not wait before turning to the three witnesses. "Let us speak, and learn from one another. For I wish to learn many things before I die and tomorrow I shall be hanged."

"We do not speak," the third witness told her.

"Our job is to listen," the second witness said.

"Can you answer a question if I ask one of you?" Adira asked.

"It is possible," the first witness admitted.

"Excellent," Adira said, "for I have a puzzle which vexes me. I have heard a tale of a cook, a seamstress, and a healer who were traveling together in the woods. Darkness fell, and the three women bedded down for the night beneath a large oak tree. Though they had a fire, it was decided that each one would take turns keeping watch lest they be attacked in their sleep.

"The cook was first. To help herself to stay awake, she took flour and water from her supply of food and mixed them together until a dough was formed. Then she shaped the dough, forming it until it took the appearance of the body of a beautiful woman. She placed the dough to bake beside the fire. She marveled at how close to life the dough seemed as it rose and grew solid in its shape. Having completed her time at watch, she woke the seamstress up to take her turn.

"The seamstress woke to find the dough risen in size and baked into a firmness so that it appeared as large and almost as real as a true woman. The seamstress did not know where it had come from, but she found herself captivated by the fine shape of the statue's face, the curve of the statue's hips, and the swell of the statue's bosom.

"So enamored was she that the seamstress took out cloth and thread. She stitched together a dress which flattered the statue's form and gave it an appearance closer to life. She stayed awake the final hours of her turn admiring the statue's beauty, then woke the healer to take the next watch.

"The statue was so lifelike that the healer was first taken with fright, thinking that a stranger had come into their campsite. Then the healer saw that it was a statue, but so beautiful a statue that she could not take her eyes off of it.

"'This is a miraculous creation,' the healer said. 'It must be given true life and not left in the dirt unadmired.'

"The healer lay down beside the statue. She warmed it with her body. She breathed air across its face. She pricked her tongue with the tip of a rose's thorn and let three drops of blood spill across the statue's lips.

"She touched the statue with her hands, massaging the arms, caressing the breasts, then moving her hands beneath the hem of the beautiful dress to tease heat into the fiery center of every woman's body.

"As she worked, the healer prayed, 'Let this perfect being come to life. Let her eyes be open, and her lungs draw breath, and let her look upon me and know that she gazes at one who will love her until the coming of Paradise.'

"The blood the healer had spilled, the skillfulness of her touch, and the pure devotion of her prayer combined to bring life into the statue's form. The statue turned into a woman with dark hair, darker eyes, and lips like ruby jewels. She felt the warm touch of the healer's hand within her and sighed her first breath, parting her thighs to let the healer further in.

"The sound was enough to waken the cook and the seamstress, however. They rose to see the statue in a woman's form. They immediately snatched the healer away, each jealously claiming that they alone had the right to possess the statue and take it to their bed. I know of this tale," Adira said, "but I do not know the solution. To whom does the woman belong?"

"That is a vexing question," the third witness agreed. "We must wait until morning and ask the counsel of the wisest in the kingdom."

"But I cannot," Adira said. "Come dawn I will be hanged. I will die not knowing the answer."

"To the third," the princess said. "For though the cook shaped her and the seamstress gave her the appearance of life, it was the third who gave the woman pleasure, and to whom the woman wishes to belong."

"Thank you for your counsel, your highness," Adira said. "I am certain you have been right each of these three nights we have been together. A wise mind, a quickening heart, and the desire to give pleasure are all sound and good reasons to shape one's choices. Were I to live one more day to see my mother and my homeland again, I would make my decisions by those methods."

"Perhaps such a thing will be possible for you," the princess said, reaching out her hand to grasp Adira's.

Adira took the princess' hand, knowing that it was her destiny that she touched. "Perhaps indeed, your highness."

And so it came to pass that the princess herself told the king and queen that she had spoken to Adira. The king and queen, having had Adira's worthiness proven to them, blessed the union of the two women and lavished many gifts upon them. The princess returned with Adira to her homeland, and they lived the rest of their lives with wisdom, love and passion.

The Seduction and Secret Life of Deirdre Fallon

Frank Fradella

June 1, 1895

Dear Diary,

I fear that Mother shall be cross with me today, lingered too long as I have in the shallows and shoals of Derrybond Waters. It was after dark before I returned, head full of cotton and eyes of dew, and her glare set nearly to put my hair on fire from the moment I stepped into the parlor. (I often wonder if I shall, when I am a mother, ever learn that look. Is it taught to one's daughter, or does one learn through sheer osmosis?)

Still and all, I must become better about standing my ground. I am not a child any longer, after all. I am seventeen, have been properly presented to society, and there is not a boy in all of London who may see the grass-stained knees of my stockings beneath my dress.

Why should she care if I spend my after-study hours in the comforting shadows of tall trees and the murmur of pleasant brooks?

But this, as you know, is all preamble, dearest Diary. I promised I would write to you again if my friend returned, and returned she has!

Oh, would that I had not lost these earlier volumes. I am certain I would have been mortified at the childish writings of my earlier years, but I would give almost anything to read my old passages of her and see how unchanged, how untouched by time she has remained.

It is magic, isn't it, Diary? Oh, I think it must be, though I try to remind myself that I am too old to believe in such things. I have poured over the scores of books in our library and have no scrap of evidence to show for it, no shred of proof to suggest that such a thing … such a girl, forgive me … may exist.

But then … then there is the rapid patter of my heartbeat, the one that remembers the laughing green of her eyes … (Oh so impossibly green! What leaf or blade of grass ever knew such colour as that?)

Oh, Diary! Am I wicked? I think I must be. Wicked, and a little mad.

Alas, Mother calls. Good night, dear Diary. Until tomorrow.

Your friend,

Abigail

June 2, 1895

Dear Diary,

I am trying not to be too heavy-hearted that my woodland friend did not, as she promised, meet me at Derrybond Waters today. How soon that I should be forced to remember the inconstancy of that sprite. My heart had only just healed from the long years of disappointment that I had suffered at her casual forgetfulness.

How long had it been between meetings, of my mysterious friend and I? Was I eight? No … nine, I think. So long that I had finally managed to convince myself that I had imagined the whole affair (and not too terribly difficult, given the omnipresent dreamlike quality she seems to engender).

But today she did not come. Not at the first faltering drop of twilight, nor (as seems to be her pleasure) at the firmer embrace of dusk. And how I strained my eyes! Darkness fell so lightly, dribbling its hue into the air around us like the falling of lazy snowflakes. I walked through the trees and spoke to the leaves (as she had once taught me to do). I dipped my fingers and toes together in the chill waters of Derrybond and still she did not come. Yet I cannot count the number of times that my senses, lent some folly by the very power of my hope, seemed to spy some sign of her. She is so like the forest itself that every whispered hush that passes through the branches sounds like her first enchanted greeting. Every babble of that brook rings on the night air like the sprinkle of her laughter. But for all my senses straining and all the mad imaginings that I allowed, there was not, at the last, any sight of her, no, nor even the slightest scent of warm apples (which accompanies her always).

Diary, I should not like to be so inconstant a friend to others as she has been to me. I believed, truly believed, that she would return today. She gave me her word, but I should have known better. How can you trust someone who won't even tell you her name?

"Names have power," she said, chiding me.

What does that mean, Diary? Power to do what?

I fear that I shall never know, and I will have no satisfaction of it tonight. I have stained the page too much with my tears for one evening. Oh, good night, sweet Diary. Until tomorrow.

Your friend,

Abigail

June 9, 1895

Dear Diary,

A week now and still no sign, no word. Were it not for her presence in the deeper waters of my dreams I might draw some breath and put these petty heartaches behind me. I surprise myself more than I may outwardly admit, waking from my slumber with my limbs leaden from those murky depths, as if my bosom were the hull of a great ship, and she my anchor.

There are winds, persistent and very of this world, that tug at my unfurled sails. And yet I remain. Unmoving. Unwilling to abandon the hope of her.

Perhaps she is more siren than anchor, and I a sailor peering into the dancing green waves, unable to look away. What shall become of me if I were to follow her into that place where mortals were never meant to tread?

For now, Diary, I can do little more than hold my breath. I feel the wash of the tides upon me. What will be left of me in a decade when she returns again?

My day beyond the woods was filled with the same books, studies and chores as it ever is. Mother has hired a piano tutor to instruct me every Thursday afternoon, and I find my fingers adept at the task. I have a good memory for patterns, and a mind just keen enough for memory. I have set aside an hour each day to practice but today the notes were flat. Lifeless.

I am weary, dear Diary. Too weary for words. Until tomorrow.

Your friend,

Abigail

June 10, 1895

Dearest Diary,

Apples!

Oh, Diary, I knew the moment I caught the scent of it in the air that she was close, so very close! I have, my entire life, been fond of the scent of apples for this very reason, that they are the harbinger of my friend. That they announce her as trumpets do the angels!

Oh, how odd my friend is, Diary. She made no apology for the promise broken, offered no reason or excuse, and indeed pretended that it was but yesterday, and not reality's half a fortnight, since she had come to Derrybond! Who is the madder of we two, I wonder?

Truth be told, Diary, I was so flush with the pleasure of finding her there that I could not bring myself to take issue with her strangeness. Is it not, I reasoned, that very *otherworldliness* that sets fire to my senses? Was it not that every imagined slight and pinprick were forgiven, nay *forgotten*, the moment she smiled at me?

Diary, I am too much in the thrall of my letters not to give a name to this … this emotion I am feeling. We are too newly met (despite that decade-old history) to call this sisterhood. I fear that all tepid traces of friendship are long since buried in the soft silt of my dreaming. Then to what name may I attribute this? What …?

Oh.

Diary.

The power of names.

I begin to understand.

Let me put that matter aside for the moment, then. Instead … no. Not tonight. Forgive me, Diary, but my revelation has left me rather speechless, and I am being a little selfish with the raw, undiluted memory of our encounter. Permit me just one more day to share these details. Tomorrow I shall set it all down, every glorious moment. For tonight, I pray you forgive me the failings of my possessive heart. (And permit me the odd sort of comfort that comes only from a friend who may not answer back.)

Until tomorrow, dearest Diary.

Your friend …

… who shall remain nameless from now on …

June 11, 1895

Dear Diary,

Fluttering in their erratic, drunken flight, those butterflies of the meadow have followed me home and taken up residence in my stomach. Their ceaseless jangle and rustling about has robbed me of any sleep and I sit here, an hour too soon for the sun to join me, to tell you of the remarkable encounter of my friend and I.

(Friend is still too small a word, Diary, but I am new to the convention of not-names and have yet to find a suitable alternative.)

She met me in the shadow of that tree, that ancient tree that must have been young when the gods had grown old, and lured me toward the darkness with a whispered greeting and the crook of her finger. I had caught the scent of her, those sweet and lovely apples, just moments before and my blood roared past my ears with so deafening a force that I did not hear her words at all. But I saw her, and felt the blush of my cheeks, and followed her into the secluded copse beyond the sight of any passerby.

We flew to each other's arms, hugging for the first time (and yet so deliciously close to the way I have dreamed it that it felt familiar), and pressed our cheeks together in a hushed hello. Her eyes were laughing, that impossible green seeming to actually glow in the darkness that held us, and we clutched hands with a nearly frantic desperation. All my idle thoughts about sirens and shipwrecks came flooding back to me then. I felt as though I had been holding my breath, yes. But not in her presence, dearest Diary. In her absence. One look at the smile which greeted me and I inhaled with all the painful joy of a newborn. Tears struggled to find purchase at the corner of my eyes and failed, spilling over, out, down onto my blushing cheeks.

She kissed me then, ever so lightly, on the tracks of those tears, and her lips were as faint and ticklish as the press of a ladybug's feet. I sighed then, audibly, and she crushed me to her bosom once more.

There will, in the course of my life, be a thousand, thousand moments worth recalling when I have breathed my last, but none so precious as this. (It will be for this reason, and this reason alone, that I shall hold you, dear Diary, more precious than any other chronicle of my life. I swear I shall let no harm befall you. Ever.)

Time passes (too quickly) and we sit in the cool bed of fallen leaves. There is something small, and vaguely lizard-like, that hops and skitters in the shadows at the edge of the tall grass but I cannot see it. My friend tells me that it is her gift for me. A new friend she would like me to meet.

"But not yet," she says. "You must wait a while first."

"Oh, but why?" I say, dragging at her hands. "You are too cruel! Please let me have it! Won't you?"

"Soon," she whispers, leaning a little closer and allowing me the full, warm weight of her scent. It is more than mere fruit, this scent of apples. It is the scent of them baked in a pie, or served warm with candied nuts. There is another scent mixed in there, something I cannot quite identify. Muskier, and a little tart.

I want to protest, to allow myself a childish stomping of feet, but her smile overrules it. There is no sadness with her, but for when we part.

"Let us play a game, you and I," she says.

"What kind of a game?" I ask.

"Close your eyes," she says. Her eyes flash that emerald fire and the mischief in her voice sits on my tongue like a new flavor.

For a moment … I am afraid. My heart races so wildly in her presence. My blood pounds in my veins. My brain, that poor lump of reason, is useless when those lips part to speak. But there is enough instinct for self-preservation that I hesitate. It was not, dear Diary, that I believed that she would harm me. But mischief is often only amusing to the giver. I did not relish the thought of being the subject of her sport. (Yes, even hers, curse my pride.)

But … then … slowly … as her smile began to vacate the warmth of that face, I found that I could refuse her nothing. I closed my eyes and waited, ears straining and the tiny hairs on my arms raising in anticipation.

There was the faint pressure of something … organic … against my lips, and the scent of apples grew stronger. Cautiously I opened my mouth, allowing her to slide the delicate slice inside, where it met my tongue. When the full taste of the apple had filled my mouth I bit down, careful to avoid those long and delicate fingers that lingered near the edge of my lips, brushing me with their tips as I chewed.

I smiled, swallowing, and she placed a second slice against my mouth, letting it rest on my lower lip as I finished. All my fears now laid to rest, I suckled at the tip of that fruit, drawing it into my mouth and letting the sensation of it wash over my tongue.

But this was not apple.

The texture, yes. The size, the shape … the same. And yet caressing my tastebuds was the sweetest mango I had ever eaten (though I had, admittedly, eaten just that one when Father took us with him to Bombay). I began to lift my lids in surprise, but she whispered to me in that voice like a spring breeze and prayed me keep them shut.

Over and over she fed me that same fruit, those crescent moons of delight, with each sliver carrying with it more delicate and odd flavours. Apple and mango and sweet chutney and honeyed almonds and raspberry tarts and things for which I have no names. Yet all with the same texture. Their shape unchanged.

With my eyes closed, the impossibility of that moment was far away, somehow removed, and I chewed on that fruit with great abandon. I parted my lips at the last to ask how such a thing was possible, to question her on the illusion she conveyed, and my mouth, apple-drenched and heavy with that nectar, blossomed like a flower to the honeybee of her kiss. My questions died in the span of that heartbeat, her hands cradling the sides of my face and her lips pressed so firmly against mine that lights burst behind my eyes.

For a moment I was stiff. This was not a friendly kiss. Not the kiss of sisters. Her mouth moved against mine, teaching me a language I had never heard, and yet some unconscious desire in me (wanton and wicked girl that I am!) spoke back. I parted my lips like the petals and found her tongue meeting mine in an act as natural as sunlight, and rain. There was shame, tiny fragments of it in the span of those moments, but they were flecks, barely more than a few drops of rain in the vastness of an ocean.

That was when I opened my eyes, dearest Diary, with our mouths lost in that wordless conversation. It was then that I saw the deep viridian hue of her skin. It was then that I saw the flowers in her hair; that hair that was green, too, but so dark as to be black. Night had fallen by then, and while my eyes were wide in the astonishment of what I saw, my hungry lips were too greedy to allow me to end their feast.

Until I noticed the wings.

They sprouted from her back, like the graceful panes of a butterfly, but dipped in moonlight and the dew of summer mornings. I gasped, opening my mouth to inhale, and her kiss deepened. My eyelids fell, the whole of my being overwhelmed by the power of her adoration.

There was no thought for me. Not then. Not for long minutes as her mouth sealed against mine and our tongues writhed against each other like the bodies of two serpents locked in battle.

At least she released me, breathless, and I blinked to find those colors gone. No wings. No tiny wreaths of daisies in her locks. Vanished. Illusion. No skittering thing in the darkness.

And then she stood up, grinning madly, and dropped the apple core to the ground.

"Tomorrow," she said, still smiling. And ran off into the woods.

Is it any wonder, dearest Diary, that I cannot sleep?

I shall write again later, dearest Diary, after I have seen her once more. Until then, pray that I may perform my chores well enough for Mother to allow me the quiet hour I crave at Derrybond.

I can still smell her in my hair …

Your friend,

… who smells of apples herself …

June 11, 1895

Dear Diary,

Again we meet by candlelight, the sun having come and gone since my earlier entry. It seems fitting that this should appear (in my journal, at any rate) as a day without sun. Without light.

She did not appear today, as I so fervently hoped she would. And yet, as heavy as my heart is, there is something in that lump of coal in my skull that has begun to glow from the heat of her passing, like the flickering ember of the fire that had once set it ablaze.

Perhaps there was no callousness in her on this last absence. Perhaps, to her mind, there *was* but one day between our meetings. I would have thought it impossible before … before I saw her wings. But now, now I have some hint as to her true nature. I am still mortal, still decidedly human, but I am a well-read human and I may tell the substance of a thing by the shape of its shadow.

I have crossed into a dangerous realm, Diary. If I am correct, my mysterious friend will return nine days hence.

Perhaps there are such things as faeries ...

Your friend,

...

June 15, 1895

Dear Diary,

When were there days ever so long as this? What is it about waiting that causes the stars in the very heavens to dig their heels in like the most stubborn of mules and strain against the yoke of Nature?

Oh, Mother is at her wit's end with me these past days. I am slow to do my chores, lethargic in the performance of my household duties, and the clanging of my hands on the delicate ivory notes has driven both her and Father to distraction. But how am I to concentrate? I ask you, Diary! All my studies seem to me to be little more than collections of random letters, strewn across the page like the up-ended box of a jigsaw puzzle. I have no powers of concentration to make them sit rightly, nor can I make any semblance of sense of them the way they are.

There are but four more days in this exile of ours. Can I stand to suffer through this over and again? Shall I be grateful that it is not, again, the decade-long absence of our first meeting?

I cannot escape the phantom flashes behind my eyes of those wings … those eyes … that kiss.

I fear there is no help for it, Diary. I am a wicked and horrible girl. I should put a halt to all this now, this very night, before I am permitted to … before these base desires consume me and move my hands to do more.

But how? How could I ever be satisfied with bland fruit and laughless breezes again?

Pray for strength for me, Diary. I have not the strength to do it myself.

Your friend,

...in turmoil...

June 19, 1895

Dearest Diary,

It is tonight. I can feel her already on the westerly winds. Already I can smell the scent of apples.

Your prayers were for naught.

Until tomorrow.

Your friend,

She Who Is Without Name

June 20, 1895

Dear Diary,

There is magic in this universe we share. Faerie magic. Bright and beautiful and terrifying and wondrous, but it exists. I have seen it. I have seen such things this night.

The sun is but an hour off and the house is silent. Mother and Father have not stirred, not made a church mouse's peep, and shall, to their dying day, not know what transpired beneath their roof this night.

Despite my last entry, the cool reason of my brain held me in check for a long hour before I could not contain myself any longer. I had sat in this room, this very chair, re-reading the words I had left behind, and thinking about the power of names. And still, I do not know what to call this.

I struggled to remain strong. I am not the child of my youth, not quite the fool that I was, but there is a human heart within me that may only be reachable by so fantastic a creature as this. This faerie-thing that has no name.

The fading dregs of the sun were leeching from the clouds and I could feel her at the edge of Derrybond Waters. Waiting. Calling to me in all but words. And there were parts of me that responded, that were set aflame in my nameless desire for her. I would not even know what to do with her if I had her but in the liquid, molten tenderness between my legs that was screaming to learn.

Without seeing her I was breathless. Tormented. I could not go. There would be no turning back for me, and I could not bear the shame of what would follow.

And yet … when the sun had expired from the skies I steadied my hand and opened my bedroom door. I could not resist her any longer. That siren call was too much to bear and I was throwing myself into the very waters that would drown me.

Suddenly she was there. At the window. Tiny as a moth, her wings flittering away, batting at the glass that separated us.

Green. She was green.

And beside her... a demon... a sprite... a creature of some other world that was half simian, half lizard. It was a tiny troglodyte, a biped, with a wide head and broad jaw that melded into its massive shoulders. And yet, for all its relative girth and muscle, the creature stood barely twelve centimeters tall. It, too, patted its paw against the glass, and I stood with my mouth agape for a long moment before I opened it.

I extended my hand to the little creature and he sniffed it cautiously before he placed a tentative paw on the fleshy part of my palm. Then he stepped fully into my hand, looked up at me and … and … I don't have the words for the plaintive little sound it made then.

"He's hungry," she said, standing fully in the middle of the room, human-colored once more, and wingless.

"What do I …?"

"Here," she said, and offered me a fingernail-sized piece of apple. I took it with my free hands and offered it to the mewling thing on my palm. He took it from me with both hands, like a squirrel, and clamped his frog-like mouth upon it.

She guided my hand to the edge of the desk and the troglodyte hopped off with his meal, taking up residence on the leather blotter where I write this now. I watched him settle onto the raised corner and chew his apple.

"What's his name?" I asked without turning around.

"What would you like it to be?"

"Chester," I said, after a moment. It seemed a cute name for a small creature such as that.

"Now pick a second," she said. Only then did I turn to face her. "Give him his *real* name. The one only the two of you know."

It was hard to think, standing there with her green eyes on me, but after a while the sound of it found its way onto my tongue and I leaned down to whisper it to him. He looked at me with his tiny black eyes unblinking and I got the distinct impression that he understood.

"And me," I said, facing her again. "Shall I have a second name as well? A real name?"

"You have a real name," she said. "That is the name that no one else must ever know. The one written on your heart. You must pick a new name for yourself. Something you will offer strangers when you meet. So long as they never know the true name of your heart, you will be safe."

"And you, who have offered me neither name? What shall I call you?"

"Come closer," she said. "I will whisper it to you."

But there were no words then. Not for many hours.

Her lips found mine and the secret name of how I felt could do nothing but allow it. I opened my mouth against hers and I felt those long, delicate fingers begin to unlace the complicated bindings that kept me clothed. Her soft tongue massaged mine, this time unhurried, passion without desperation. My skirt fell to the floor. I was powerfully aware at the sense of exposure I felt. But no shame. Not yet. Perhaps that would come later. I found my hands at her shoulders, pulling her simple, ephemeral garment away … feeling it come apart in my hands like cobwebs.

And then her fingers were inside me, gliding into me as if they'd always belonged there, my whole body accepting, even eager for it. I was aware of the dampness where her hand made contact with me, could feel the hidden flower beneath me clutch at her ministrations, but in that moment, in that breathless shock of sensation, there was no rational thought. A sound issued from my mouth, born from the depths of my soul, and I heard it echo against the hollow of her throat. She moved her fingers inside me, her other hand curled into the strands of my hair, holding me in that primal intensity of that kiss, and my hips moved of their own volition, grinding against the waves of ecstasy she was engendering. My breath became ragged, panting, and still she held me in that kiss, locked against her mouth though my tongue now, like my hips, did not act on any order from me.

I clung to her so tightly that I feared I might hurt her, but then … then there was no more thought. I felt the wave swell … rise … crest … and shatter with devastating force on the shore of my womanhood. My whole being shuddered, my cries swallowed by the faerie who had brought them forth, and my legs buckled beneath me.

She caught me, just barely, and we sidled to the bed with her fingers still dripping from the evidence of my weakness.

The last shreds of my garments fell away and we lay side by side while I trembled in the aftershocks. Her hands never stopped moving, never ceased caressing me. Her fingertips played at the tips of my nipples, her palms hefting the weight of my breasts. But when she lowered her head, when the first breath of her washed over them, my back arched involuntarily and she covered the circle of my left nipple with her mouth. Nothing beyond that was a conscious thought. I became a creature of pure instinct. Pure need. I rolled over on top of her and pinned her to the bed. I dipped my head down and ran my mouth along the strong line of her neck. I felt her hands on my back, felt the sharp stab of her nails, and it only spurred me on.

"No illusions," I whispered in her ear. "No more glamours."

And when I pulled away her flesh, her delicious, immortal flesh, was that deep emerald hue once more. She smiled, looking up into my face, and I smiled back at her before lowering myself to devour her once more.

I was trembling, both in fear and anticipation, when my hand flowed over the contour of her stomach … down across the small rise of her hips … and into the valley of her sex. There was a river there, warm and waiting, and she moaned as I dipped my fingers into that steaming pool. I curled my fingers in that same "come here" gesture to which she had invited me into the shadows and I felt my own need rise again as she bucked and whimpered beneath my hand.

Distant and far away, the worry that my parents might overhear us found me and I covered her mouth with me, feeling her cries find their home in the butterfly garden of my belly. She gasped and pushed against my hand, and I could feel the sudden rise of that wave overtake her by the clenching around my fingers, and the geyser-like spill of her passion.

Side by side we faced one another, drowning in the endless torrent of kisses and tiny nibbles on shoulder, on earlobes, on the more tender flesh that lies lower.

She inverted herself, her mouth covering the swollen lips between my legs, then straddled me to offer her own hidden passion. Trembling, still trembling, I raised my head and we clung to one another in a Möbius Strip of bliss.

And somewhere, past the portents and the passion, beyond my shame and utter joy, I found a name for myself on the tip of my tongue, as if it had been birthed there by the sweet, musky taste of my lovely faerie.

Deirdre Fallon. That shall be my name.

I tell you this, Diary, because you, and only you, can be trusted with such a secret. On the morrow I depart for the faerie hills, leaving the tedium of this life forever.

She says she will teach me the magic of the apples. She promises to teach me many things. I can hardly wait.

Farewell, dear Diary. I shall hide you well before I go.

Your friend,

Deirdre

Sleeping Beauty, Indeed

Regan M. Wann

The baying of the hounds and the calling of the men
Cannot bring her sleep to waking again
I've vouched her safe and locked the gate
As for you all, naught to do but ... wait.

It was not the prick of a spindle that brought us to this place. Oh no. It was a pricking of a very different sort, the kind which young women of royal blood need not know prior to the marriage bed.

Not that anyone actually prescribes to that. Virtue is not what it used to be, or if I am honest, what it has never been. I have seen many generations of royalty come through this fortress of stone, of many bloodlines, and none have been, shall we say, paragons of virtue or of faith. Bored people with nothing to do but eat and rut to while the hours.

We Faery are of a different ilk. We border on incorporeal, which can be very useful when one is tied in service to humankind. Necessary. It keeps everything so much tidier.

My service to the princess in question came at her christening. I was late. It is as simple as that. Time is so fluid for Faery, often one of Us forgets where We are promised. It is like drawing straws, the one of Us who arrives last, well, She is thus tied to the Godchild in a more solid sense than the rest. So it was my turn again.

To be fair, I had not taken a true Godchild in many human lifetimes. I was more than due. So I sighed, and resigned myself to a half century or so of servitude. Little did I know; We Faery may know more than humankind, but We cannot see the future.

After a perdurable meal in which seemingly every noble, major or minor, to be found within a week's travel stood to speak of the glory that was the howling girl-child, We Faery were finally brought to the bassinette to offer our ethereal gifts. We were twelve in number, and as the Godmother, I was given the honor of bestowing the final gift.

Tiny child of lineage great
Let Faery folk attend your fate
A life so blessed our gift to you
Thus we begin, without ado

One:
Beauty without surcease
Two:
Her brow no frown shall crease
Three:
Wit and laughter gay
Four:
Never shall she lose her way
Five:
Joyful light shines from her core
Six:
Hope and wisdom evermore
Seven:
Charming appeal to all she meets
Eight:
Vision to see to all her needs
Nine:
Ability to learn and grow
Ten:
A mind within ideas to sow
Eleven:
Deep within a gentle soul

From the back of the packed chamber came a chilling voice, *"Twelve, her sex a gaping hole!"* paired with a devilish cackling.

I sighed inwardly as the entire company turned on this interruption. The king turned crimson and his wife went pale. The baby simply laughed and cooed.

"Thought you could escape inviting old Fama, did you? Well, Fama comes invited or no! Fama will not be denied. Fama has gifts to give, blessings for all. Even for Fama's wicked, wicked sisters who do not love her. Her sisters should show Fama respect, or Fama's tongue will turn to lashings, and wicked sisters do not like the lashings!"

As the Godmother, even without having given my own blessing, it was my job to appease her. Fama is not Our sister, We are not certain she is even Faery, although she is clearly kin. We think of her as more like a distant cousin. One whose family has known their own siblings a little too well in trying to keep the bloodline whole.

As the king gawped like an air-drowned fish, it was clear that something needed to be done, and quickly. I stepped forward and bowed low to Fama.

"Sister-cousin, We meant no disrespect. Please accept Our humble atonement and give Us the courtesy of your continued company this Faery-year."

Several of my Sisters gasped. A Faery-year was quite a long time in human terms, and while it would mean hardship on my Sisters, it would appease Fama and keep her out of the way of this family, allowing the girl to grow into adulthood without the already cast blessing coming to a dangerous fruition. If I understood Fama, which I like to think I did, this invitation was the one she was truly seeking, not an invitation to the christening of a human girl-child.

"Mmmmm, Fama thinks she is being appeased, yes? Fama thinks maybe not this time. Fama thinks she would like to take her own place as Godmother. Fama thinks it has been too long that Faery-folk have lived in manors among human-kind. Fama thinks Fama deserves the same gifts, honors and dues!"

I sighed inwardly again, this time at the ridiculous futility of it all. If only Fama could take my place, I would happily give it to her, damn the consequences. Once Our spell was started, all we Sisters speaking together, I was tied for life to the little human beast. Fama, exempt from Our charm, could not have taken my place under any circumstance. However, she could be difficult to be rid of and could not be dealt with lightly. Like vermin, or the pox, one must apply just the right remedy or one would be stuck with Fama for a human lifetime.

At this point the king found his voice.

"Uhrm … uh … great and wondrous Fama, please accept this human's most sincere apology for an invitation lost in the frenzy of this, the birth of our first child. We honor your presence and hope that you will honor our daughter with your good will." And with that, he bowed low, causing everyone in the room to follow suit.

I saw her soften as the room offered her homage.

"Mmmm … Fama will join the Faery for one Faery-year, yes. Then Fama will return, and will expect appropriate honor! Do not forget Fama!" With a crack, she disappeared, taking my Sisters with her.

Helpless, the parents stood and looked at me.

"Will the, um, will the charm she gave our daughter, the blessing … will it stick?"

"Like ivy to your walls, I am afraid, my king and queen. However, I have not yet given my blessing. It will take some further trouble than we might hope, but I will not let your daughter succumb to a life of harlotry. Fear not."

I approached the child and looked deeply into her chestnut eyes. Right.

Thirteen:

A simple blessing, meant for good
To hold on fast, as strong as wood

This child may be smart and wild
But let her honor not be defiled
Should her maiden come to harm
Bring about my chosen charm
Close the doors and shut the eyes
Sleep descends on all she spies
Until her lover, so true and fair
Wakes her with a kiss, beyond compare

The king and queen looked gratefully at me, and I resigned myself for a long and challenging ride.

The child was sweet, I will be fair about that. Easy to care for, never a problem for her nurses or maids. Really, the problem didn't begin until she began to walk. Her wetnurse noticed it first.

"Mistress Faery, I've taken to notice the bairn spends a lot of time, well, focused on her nether regions, if you catch my drift, ma'am."

"I do, Mistress Nurse, and I can tell you that we will need to curtail this behavior quickly, to teach her where and when she may partake of her pleasure, and where and when she may not do so."

"M'lady?"

"Just do as I say, she will not be stopped so she must be educated."

"But …"

"Please, take my word on this one, Mistress Nurse."

"Yes, ma'am."

Thus was the child trained to her own bedchamber when the urge to touch was upon her. This functioned quite well for some time. She spent a great deal of time alone, but she was a happy child, able to attend to her own needs in her own ways.

Then the age of playmates descended upon us all. Suddenly we became aware of a new threat to her maidenhead: other children.

All boys were hastily removed from her circle. After much discussion, her mother, nurse and myself determined that girls were of no danger to her delicate chastity.

To suggest that she wore her fellow playmates out is certainly an understatement. The fun of a partner was beyond all kenning. As the family of the highest status within more than a week's journey, it was the young princess' will to take who she would into her intimate confidence.

Girls of this region married young in this generation, younger than three generations before or after. Their eyes were opened to a new world, one which was hard to deny. In this way the princess was heir to a fruitful community, a side effect no one saw coming but which was not, ultimately, a negative thing.

Sadly, the same was true of our princess. I did not see it coming, but one day it was upon us, with nothing to do but hope for the best.

I was observing, as was my wont, from a quiet corner of the room. The girls were not even aware of my presence. To be completely honest, I was not being as attentive as I should have been. I was lost in thoughts of Faery, of home and Sisters and the day that I would be freed from human service again.

Enclosed with her dearest friend, a bright young woman named Melony, the princess was a bit more forceful than usual. They must have been experimenting with their hands, and our princess worked her entire hand inside her writhing playmate. As she explored, turning her fingers this way and that to feel all the workings of her beloved companion, all the while continuing to stroke and minister with her free hand, something happened that surprised them both. Melony felt a building inside unlike anything she had ever felt. Her breathing became shallow and ragged and her eyes closed tight. As the rising increased, she moved against her friend's hand faster and with more intensity, exciting the princess horribly. With a sudden shout she wrenched her hips high and curled her toes, then relaxed.

"What happened?" Melony asked, looking dreamily into the eyes of her dear princess.

"I have no idea. Try me!"

Melony was only too happy to comply. With much giggling and questioning, "Was it like this, or perhaps this?" the princess found her own breathing beginning to become harsher. She knew this feeling, she had brought herself to relief many times on her own, but never with another person. This was something new, something wonderful. She never wanted it to end. She tried desperately to prolong the inevitable, but could not and finally succumbed with a shuddering sigh.

When Melony removed her hand, it was covered in sticky blood. Both she and the princess stared for a long moment, still basking in pleasure but with a taste of fear just beginning around the edges.

"Why, what … you didn't have that, why not?" Melony had no answer for her friend. She considered the young men of the stables that she often frolicked with and did remember blood on one of the early encounters.

"I don't …" At that very moment the clouds furiously approached. I felt the change, smelled the storm roll in, and knew we were all in trouble.

I flew to the princess, reaching the girls almost at the same moment as the nurse entered the chamber. I was gripping Melony's bloody hand and felt horror begin to dawn. We both looked at the confused girls as reality sunk in. We thought we had been so careful, so cautious. Clearly we had not been cautious enough.

"Hurry," I said to the flustered nurse, "get her parents, her maids, get her dog … quickly!"

The nurse looked at me as if I was mad. Perhaps I was, a bit. I glared at her and snapped, "Now!"

She scurried off like I had struck her. I watched her go, then grabbed Melony harshly and shook her, as if my words could physically penetrate her brain that way.

"You fool, don't you know what you have done?" The frightened girl began wailing and I took pity. "Anyway, you need to go, quickly, run home as fast as you can. Do not tell anyone what you have seen or done today. Wash your hand clean of that blood. Stop crying now, it will all be alright."

She washed her hand and scuttled from the room. I turned to the princess.

"Well, this is certainly unexpected. Hurry, into your best gown and into bed! We haven't a moment to lose."

She looked at me as if I were speaking a different language. I glared at her and spoke in a more direct, clipped manner, "Get … dressed … and … get … back … into … the … bed, you ninny!"

She was beginning to be frightened, but she did as she was bade. Fine. Her family was entering the room, looking just as bewildered and frightened. Good, that would help them to do as I asked.

"Right, her maidenhead has been compromised. My charm is already set in motion. There's no time to explain, just get comfortable. I'll explain, uh, later." I didn't tell them I expected later to be an entire human lifetime or so.

Once the king and queen, her little dog, favorite maids and of course, her loyal nurse, were assembled and made comfortable, the princess settled herself drowsily into her pillows.

"I'm so tired. Why am I so tired?"

"Shhh, don't worry, Godchild. Sleep, and all will be well."

She slipped into dreams as the horrified room watched, still reeling from what I had told them. I smiled gently and made my way around the room, caressing each on the startled face.

"Sleep, sleep and all will be well. Worry not. Worry not." They all fell immediately into a deep slumber.

I hurried out of the room and sent away the remainder of the staff. I will admit, they received handsome reward for their sudden dismissal, so none left unhappily. I encouraged them to take all perishables from the manor. No one argued. I closed all the gates and turned all the locks. I filled the moat with water dragons. I caused the ivy to grow until the tall towers were nearly obscured. I left very little to chance.

Verily, I expected at least twenty human years to pass before the queue began to kiss the princess and see who her one true love might be. It was only two years, and they lined up like ducks. Men from all walks of life, who had heard her story in their nurseries or in their barrooms, fantastical tales of her beauty, sensuality and wealth, all to be won for the cost of a kiss. Word travels so fast when a dowry like hers is at stake.

There was much more to do with this constant stream of manhood coming through the door. I must protect the princess and remain with her at all times. I must not allow the waiting men to ransack the manor, steal the silver, and meddle with the sleeping family. They were not to be rough with the princess when she did not wake for them, nor attempt to kiss in other ways, as I learned when I stepped back into the room after a short respite to find a minor noble with his head under her skirts.

After sleeping a full five years—three of them with a constant stream of would-be suitors—I found myself frustrated, bored and annoyed for having thought of such a stupid solution. I should have left her to Fama's curse, damn the consequences. My intention had been to bless her with good sense. Surely that would have led her down a path of sexual promiscuity (one that many of her peers also walk) but with sense enough to keep it private. But no, I had to intervene and appear to preserve her chastity, which was never mine to preserve and hardly worth the effort. I was weary of my charge and weary of kisses, weary of men and certainly weary of the continued sleep of my Godchild.

I will admit I was getting lax in my duties. I was bored, and I was not paying enough attention to who was entering the door of the bedchamber. As the feet padded across the thick, yet now worn rugs I didn't even look up from my hands as I said, "One kiss, simply on the lips, and do not handle her roughly. Right. Off you go. And leave the dog alone."

The change was immediate. It was the sun coming out from behind thick clouds. It was dawn. It was glorious. I raised my eyes to see the lucky man who would win her heart and my eyes met a familiar face.

I will admit, I was shocked.

"Melony?" She curtsied and blushed, but her smile was wide as she watched her lady wake from her long slumber.

"I have always loved her, Faery Godmother. How can that be wrong? I have thought of no one since your charm separated us." I considered, the girl might be on to something there. "And look, at my kiss she rises. I am her one true love. I was certain that must be the case."

The reunion was quite joyful. The princess seemed a little confused by the seemingly overnight aging of her playmate and Melony kept stroking the unchanged cheeks of my charge, showering her with kisses and tears. There was no question that this was a match of love, if not of convenience.

My mind raced as I tried to take in what I was seeing, tried to force myself to figure out what the next step could possibly be. I heard a crack and was surrounded suddenly by my Sisters, come to help. Fama came with them.

As my Sisters encircled me and offered comfort, Fama stalked the room and looked deeply into the faces of the sleeping family and servants. She looked at the girls, who saw only each other. Finally, she looked at We Faery and cocked her head like a bird spying a fat worm.

"Mmmm … Fama has much enjoyed the Faery hospitality, but Fama thinks perhaps she is ready for her human time."

I looked at her, aghast. What could she mean by that?

"Fama, I don't understand …"

"Mmmm, no? Of course Faery do not understand! Fama is here for a reason, here for one thing only. To take Fama's rightful place in the human time."

As my Sisters and I watched, Fama began to spin on the spot. She spun so fast We could no longer see her. When she finally slowed, she was identical to the still sleepy princess.

"Mmmm, yes, Fama will take her place. Princess and Love will be free to go … go to the World, go to Faery, but *go*! Mmm, yes, it is the only way for there to be a happily ever after, Fama thinks. What thinks Faery?"

My Sisters and I glanced uneasily around the room, at Fama, at the young women on the bed with the light of love in their eyes. I stepped forward.

"Yes, Fama, I believe you may be right."

"Fama knows. Hah! And Fama will wait until the *most* handsome one comes for kisses and caresses! Yes, Fama will be alright and so will Princess and Love, after all."

With great gentleness I raised the princess and Melony from the bed and asked them if they would be content to join us for a Faery-year, together. The princess caught up Melony's hand, laughing, and said without a single hesitation, "If we are together, we will go anywhere in the World or Faery. Please, yes, let us go!"

Fama took her place, and lying there as if asleep she looked very like the princess had. I wondered what the poor man who she chose was likely to think of his unusual bride once he woke her. And would the King and Queen know this was not their daughter?

Little matter. We took the women to Faery where they lived until their natural lives were ended. They lived in joy and filled with love. And if the story books are to be believed, Fama finally woke and took her prince. I know we have neither heard nor seen her since. I can only assume that she joined the human time and lived her life, happily ever after.

Future Fortunes

Kori Aguirre-Amador

"Do you think he can do it?" the Fortune Teller cackled, her bright yellow and broken teeth flashing from behind her old, cracked lips. "Do you really?"

The Prince was in no mood for her prodding, however. "Why don't you tell me? If you can really see the future, that is."

"Fortune and future are rare bedfellows," the Fortune Teller cackled again.

"What the hell does *that* mean?" the Prince spat.

"In the end, you'll be able to answer that for yourself," the Fortune Teller pulled out a deck of Tarot cards. "How confident are you that he'll succeed? Not very, I take it," she answered before giving him a chance to reply. "If you've come to me, you can't be too confident in your mercenary."

"Shuffle the cards, old woman," the Prince demanded.

"Is that a threat?"

"You tell me," the Prince leaned back in his seat enough to reveal the hilt of his sheathed sword. "Is it your fortune or your future?" He had little patience for the Fortune Teller anymore. Even though he had been a faithful customer of hers since he was a child dreaming of great deeds and fortunes beyond what he had been born into. She had always told him what he wanted to hear.

She had told him that he would become a great warrior. And so had he become one of the most renowned warriors in Persia. So renowned, that the king openly paid homage to him, the son a merchant. The Fortune Teller had told him that he would lead thousands upon thousands of men to their doom and glory in a great number of wars. And so he had. He became a general in his own right. The men he led were not the king's but his own. His personal army that followed him and him alone to doom and glory.

She had told him that he would gain status. And he had. The King of Persia recognized him, dined with him, shared secrets with him, asked advice from him. He had even used his status to convince the king to give him one of the princesses in marriage. The Fortune Teller hadn't predicted this; he had made his own future and fortune and become a Prince.

Then she gave him a bad fortune, and that is when his patience with her began to wane. She told him that the king had betrayed him. His princess would never be a wife to him. In fact, she was destined to never know the touch of a man. The new Prince had been furious with the Fortune Teller. He had screamed, ranted, called her a fraud in public as his entire world crashed around him.

The king had heard the same fortune; from the moment she was born he had been told of her fate. Hearing that his daughter should never know the touch of a man, he locked the young woman away in the highest floor of the highest tower known to mankind. He had never held his daughter when she was a baby, nor had he ever even visited her tower. No men were allowed in the tower, the princess lived on the highest floor and had never left her room in her life. She was well-guarded by the finest female warriors he could buy. Giving up one daughter was nothing compared to the price of tempting the fates.

When the Prince learned of this, the king conveniently severed ties with him. When he appeared in court, he was ignored. When he asked for an audience, he was treated as the son of a merchant and not as a son-in-law of the king. To make matters worse, the marriage had not been annulled; the king made it clear that he liked the Prince's ineffectual position. Even he would have a difficult time in convincing his troops to attack his own father-in-law, yet he would never be able to produce a royal heir to challenge the king's grandsons.

And so the Prince began to see how everything he had worked so hard to obtain was about to fall apart. He enjoyed his new status but even more so he enjoyed his fast mobility through the ranks of the kingdom. He had made it as far as the rank of prince, and he didn't plan to stop there. But the first step, was to regain control of the princess.

"And that's where the Horseborn comes in," the Fortune Teller lifted the top card off the tarot deck It was the ten of swords. "Violence," she announced. She set the card down on the table. The picture was of a warrior, impaled by ten swords with bright red blood painted on the blades. She closed her eyes and opened the part of her brain which usually lay dormant until subconsciousness allowed it some limited freedom.

The Horseborn was a warrior from far to the east and north of their land. He was renowned for breaking the Great Wall of the Qin. It was said that he slew over a thousand Qin warriors with one spear and then feasted upon their remains. The Fortune Teller would liked to have believed this was pure hyperbole, but she saw the warrior in the card.

He was riding on a small horse of the steppe, leaning so far forward in the saddle he was practically lying down on the beast's neck. He pulled a short, curved sword out so fast the Fortune Teller hadn't seen the motions. The first line of defense for the princess was a line of Persians warriors; they were all male and were outside the tower, encircling it.

Sunlight glinted off of the finely-honed edge of the curved sword as the Horseborn lifted it over his head. The horse charged straight into the warriors, but before they had enough time to react, the curved blade swooped down.

Suddenly, in the time it would take to blink an eye, the Horseborn was on the opposite side of the ring of warriors and at least ten of them had died where they stood. The remaining warriors were in shock; they stared not at the eastern warrior but at their fallen comrades.

That proved to be a mistake.

The curved blade gleamed red now in the sunlight, and as the Horseborn charged, the warriors fell. Not a single one of the king's finest had managed to draw his sword in the princess' defense.

The Fortune Teller gasped.

"What?" the Prince demanded. He leaned forward over the table, staring at the card. "What does it mean?"

The Fortune Teller pulled a shaking hand away from the card she had left face up. "It means what I said," she tried to regain her composure as she reached for another card. "It means violence."

"Good," the Prince grunted. "I didn't pay an exorbitant amount of money for him to talk his way into the princess' tower."

The Prince had certainly gotten his money's worth; this Horseborn was exceptional. The Fortune Teller looked down, hiding an involuntary smile from the temperamental prince. Exceptional people often had this tendency to be the most unpredictable as well.

She pulled a second card from the top of the deck. She held it up so only she could see it. The nine of wands. "Strength," she whispered.

"What?" the Prince was still looking at the ten of swords card on the table.

"Strength," the Fortune Teller said slightly louder. She stared hard at the card. At the figure depicted therein, a man holding a staff, surrounded by eight other staffs. At the Horseborn who had just defeated over a dozen of the king's best.

The Horseborn looked over the dead warriors. It seemed so easy. Surely the king had better, more challenging protection for his prize than this. He had his horse trot around the circumference of the tower, looking for an entrance. There was nothing but plain mud bricks.

He dismounted and walked the circumference on foot, examining it closely. There was still no sign of door or window. There wasn't so much as a crack in the nearly seamless bricks. Impossible. Even the Fortune Teller was confused. The princess lived inside the tower, along with guards and servants. *She* might not be allowed outside the tower, but what about her staff? The guards and servants must have some, however limited, means of coming and going, if for no other reason than to bring food and water to the princess.

The Horseborn looked up as he walked around the tower once more. He mentally counted a hundred paces upward; there was a window there. No more than a slit, it was the type of window built for the arrows of archers. Even at that distance, the Horseborn could tell it was too small to fit a fully grown person in it. Besides, the window was too high. He had done many things in the course of his life: He had raided the western steppe, broken the wall of Qin, swam a freezing river to land where gold lay unprotected and undiscovered on the open ground. But he had never flown, and he wasn't likely to figure out how to accomplish that feat now.

He needed to play to his strength.

He put a hand on the brick, and then walked slowly around the circumference of the tower again. This time very, very slowly. He finished one circuit. Then he moved his hand down, feeling another brick, then the brick next to it, and then the next. And so on until he had completed another circuit.

The Horseborn repeated this process until he found what he was looking for. One brick that was slightly loose. Most likely, this one brick had received a fraction less mortar than the rest. Normally, a builder would not think twice about this slight mistake. And normally, it would not be a fatal one. However, this was exactly the type of mistake the Horseborn had experience with.

He stepped back from the tower and quickly calculated the loose brick's place inside it. He concentrated, knowing that his strike had to be perfect. After a moment of meditation, he was ready. One quick step, then he jumped and kicked. His foot hit the brick sideways, striking it dead center, and the Horseborn could feel the results.

The brick was pushed inside, leaving a hole in the tower. With the hole, the Horseborn was able to make some real progress. He pulled out his sword, but left it sheathed. He stuck the weapon in the hole and used it as a lever to wedge an adjacent brick free. And then another adjacent brick, and then another, and another. Until he had a hole he could fit through.

Then the Horseborn was inside the tower.

"Amazing strength," the Fortune Teller finally set the nine of wands down, face up, on the table.

"As I said," the Prince stifled a yawn, "I paid for strength. I expect it."

Something about this told the Fortune Teller that the Prince should not expect to know anything about the Horseborn. She pulled another card off the top of the deck. It was the death card. "Transformation," she breathed. "What can this mean?" she muttered lowly to herself.

The Prince stared as she set the card down on the table top face up. He visibly whitened.

"This means something will change," the Fortune Teller explained. "Not necessarily that someone will die." Her hand remained on the card even after she had placed it in the spread. She closed her eyes and saw with a different set.

The tower was poorly lit and the air was stale. The Horseborn had adopted the Persian nomad style of headdress that covered the face, for which he was now grateful as it keep the dust from his nose and mouth. A spiral staircase wound up the tower and the Horseborn wasted no time.

As he made his way up the stairs, he noticed that he would occasionally pass a slit window, big enough for an archer to use but too small for anyone other than an underfed child to fit through. There were no other holes or openings in the tower. The windows were also the only light source, as there were no torches or holders for torches.

Halfway up the stairs, the Horseborn saw a shadow. He stopped immediately and drew his curved blade.

He watched the shadow tensely. It had to be something outside the tower. The shadow passed over the top of the Horseborn, disappeared for a moment and then reappeared around the curve of the spiral staircase. He had not been able to study the shape for any great amount of time, but it had looked like it had wings.

He kept his sword out and proceeded up the staircase with caution. It had to be a bird—something with wings and something small enough to fit in the windows. He heard a thud. Then a scraping sound, like claws against the stone stairs. Whatever it was, it was definitely inside the tower now.

The Horseborn knew he had no reason to fear a bird, but caution was always safer than confidence, and so he kept his curved blade drawn and proceeded slowly. He walked with his back outside the outer edge of the spiral staircase so he would have a full view of the bird when he rounded the corner.

He was tense and ready for action. Until he saw the bird. It was an unremarkable creature, a small raptor with brown coloring. Next to it lay a cloth bundle that was nearly the same size if not larger than the bird itself.

The Horseborn relaxed his guard. Only a bird, nothing to worry about. His sword dropped slightly.

That was all it took.

Before he knew it, the Horseborn found himself slammed into the outer wall of tower with such force that he lost his balance and tumbled down the hard, stone steps. By the time he had regained his balance enough to stop himself from falling further, another blow struck him and he tumbled down more stairs. Every time he regained enough composure to stand upright, another blow would knock him off his feet sending him further and further down the stair case.

Until he reach the bottom.

Finally, the Horseborn was able to wobble to his feet in enough time to dodge the upcoming blow. His vision was blurred from dizziness and all he saw at first was a streak of brown running past him. He barely managed to dodge out of its path, and it clipped him, disrupting his newly regained balance, but it did not knock him off his feet.

The Horseborn whirled around, looking both for his attacker and for the sword he realized had fallen from his grip. For a moment, he saw neither. But soon he realized that was only because he had assumed his attacker was human.

On the far side of the circular tower was a wolf. It was in a half crouch, ready to pounce and baring its teeth.

The Horseborn slowly reached for his left boot with his left hand. Wolves generally only attacked when provoked, so if he moved slowly and carefully enough, it shouldn't feel threatened enough to attack him. So the Horseborn watched the wolf warily, careful not to make direct eye contact and careful not to make his movements look threatening.

But before his hand could reach the dagger sheathed on his ankle, the wolf pounced again. He ducked and rolled sideways. The Horseborn knew wolves had poor peripheral vision and that it should not have seen him.

The wolf, however, did see him. As soon as it landed in the spot where the Horseborn had been, it turned on a dime and pounced again. This time the Horseborn did not have enough time to dodge. The wolf hit him square in the chest, knocking him to the earthen floor. The

Horseborn flung his arms over his head, scant protection that it was, and the wolf didn't miss the opportunity to sink its long canines into his forearm.

He grunted with pain, and paled slightly at the sight of his own blood dripping down the wolf's jawline. But he didn't miss his opportunity, either. He twisted his arm, pulling the wolf's jaws and head along with it, and rolling over onto his side. From that position, the Horseborn was able to connect a viscous kick to the side of the animal's head.

It surprised the wolf enough that its grip on the Horseborn's arm weakened. He wrenched his arm out of its jaws, tearing the wound open, but at least he was free. He connected another kick while the beast was still startled and in the same motion, pulled his dagger from his ankle sheath.

The wolf was thrown off the Horseborn and against the tower's wall.

The Horseborn almost forgot the dagger in his hand as he watched in transfixed horror.

The wolf's back nearly connected with the stone wall, but it had managed to twist itself around in the air so that its feet would hit instead of the back. The padded feet touched the wall, and then flattened, the feet became longer as did the toes and the sole. Then the legs thickened, the fur grew longer and sleeker. The back elongated, the neck and muzzled shortened.

The Horseborn remembered the dagger and looked at it as he tightened his grip. When he looked up again, he was no longer facing a wolf but a bear. The bear grunted as it rolled onto its feet, but besides that, made no other noises. Not even a growl.

The Horseborn scampered to his feet, felt the knife's weight and threw it before either he or the bear could think about it. It was the only way he could defeat a bear, to use the element of surprise.

The bear made no sound when the knife embedded itself in its chest. The Horseborn prepared himself for the raging wrath of an injured animal, but instead faced a silent, calm bear whose only reaction was to look down and regard the knife newly embedded in the left side of its ribcage.

The Horseborn backed away from it. Something wasn't right. The animal had transformed from a wolf to a bear, but beyond that, it did not act as an animal should. This was more than an enchanted wolf.

The bear reached for the knife with a paw. The claws of which appeared to shrink, the hair receded and the finger elongated even more. The arms lengthened, the bones becoming thinner and more delicate as the hair receded further and further up the hand and then the arm. Soon the bear was nearly hairless, the limbs were long and delicate, the muscles were fine and no longer thick and powerful.

The figure slumped forward, betraying its first effect of the injury.

The Horseborn was torn between wanting to run up the stairs and fear of turning his back on a proven dangerous creature.

He took a tentative step towards it.

The creature lifted its head. The Horseborn froze where he stood. It was a human now, a woman tall and strongly built with exotic blond hair and pleading blue eyes. He took one more step towards her, but she fell to the ground with a jerk. Blood stained the earth floor, and one long arm reached from her wound to his feet. The arm was as soaked with blood as the floor and in her hand was the Horseborn's dagger. She made no more movements past that.

He carefully reached down and delicately pried the dagger from her already cold hand. He didn't bother to wipe it clean. He ran up the staircase pausing only to retrieve his curved sword. He was at the top, the entrance to the princess' chamber, in no time.

The Fortune Teller tapped the death card. "Transformation," she said quietly.

"What?" the Prince demanded.

"The Horseborn has reached the princess," the Fortune Teller told him. "He has passed all her guards."

"Everything is as expected," the Prince smiled. He had been concerned for a moment. Maybe his plans wouldn't work, maybe the king would have the last laugh after all. But his mercenary had come through for him. All would be right again soon. He stood. He had no more use for the wizened Fortune Teller.

"There are two more cards," the Fortune Teller protested.

"Can two cards change the fate you've already told me?" The Prince doubted it.

"Every card changes fate," the old woman reached for another. She showed it to the Prince before she looked at it herself. "What card is it?""

The Prince leaned over the top of the table, disrupting the face up cards slightly. He squinted. It was woman, dressed in gaudy clothing and holding something. "The Queen of ..." He squinted again.

The Fortune Teller closed her eyes.

The Horseborn had made it into the princess' chamber. Maids were screaming, yet none offered any sort of substantive defense for their princess. The Horseborn didn't deign to consider any of them. They were not his concern.

She was seated on a sofa which was situated next to undoubtedly the largest window of the tower. She stared out of the window, seemingly lost in her own world.

The Horseborn, for his part, was bleeding profusely from the bite on his arm. He was rapidly losing patience with this princess, even though they had never met. He grabbed her roughly by the shoulder, turning her around to face him.

She did not flinch at his violence, but instead stared up him. Her face was covered, every inch of it except for the eyes. Her eyes had the same pleading quality as the shape-changing woman had. The Horseborn was still holding her shoulders; he did not let go, but he stared into her eyes realizing that they had more depth than he ever would have considered. She reached up gently and pulled the nomadic head scarf from his face.

"Interesting," the Fortune Teller muttered.

"You haven't even seen the card," the Prince took the card from her hand and showed to her. "What does it mean? The Horseborn has the princess? This card doesn't change that."

"This card only confirms it," the Fortune Teller took the card and held it for a moment.

"It's not a Queen," she explained. "It's the Princess of Disks."

"The Princess …" the Prince smiled. Everything was going to work, his worrying was over.

"A young woman … and change," the Fortune Teller explained.

"Many things are going to change for the princess," the Prince grinned and pulled out two gold coins for the Fortune Teller. He tossed them nonchalantly on her table, on top of the Tarot spread. He then left without so much as a good-bye.

His future and fortune were both assured. He had the princess, and with her in his control, he would have the king soon enough. He untethered and mounted his horse. He was going to meet the Horseborn outside the tower and take his prize at the soonest possible moment.

The Fortune Teller watched the Prince leave. There was one more card, but she doubted he would want to see it. She set the Princess of Disks down in the spread. No, he definitely would not want to see it. He wouldn't want to know that there was more than one young woman the Princess of Disks could refer to. She set her hand on the deck and closed her eyes again.

The princess held the Horseborn's head scarf and stared into his face. The Horseborn let go of her shoulders and stumbled backward, covering his face with his hands.

"What sort of secret could you possibly have?" the princess asked. As she spoke, she took note of the bite of the Horseborn's forearm. Her eyes moistened. "You defeated my guards … all of them." She looked down to the floor and didn't face her new capturer again until she had composed herself. "*You* have nothing to fear."

The Horseborn fumbled for his headcloth, still covering his face.

"You should know that it has been said I will never know the touch of a man," the princess swallowed heavily. "I am prepared to guarantee that fate will not be tempted." She pulled a serrated dagger from a fold in her dress. She raised her hand and pointed the dagger toward herself. She knew well that she could never defeat a man who had bested her trusted shape-changing body guard. The only option she had left to her was to end her own life instead of making a futile attempt to end his.

The Horseborn forgot about his face and intercepted the princess' dagger before she hit her mark.

The princess struggled against her capturer's grip, but it was all in vain. She wondered how fate could be mocked like this as the Horseborn held her hand by the wrist and moved close to her body to balance. In no time, he had wrenched the dagger free. It clanged where it dropped on the floor.

The Horseborn made no pretense towards delicacy as he searched the princess for more hidden weapons. The princess still could not believe fate had abandoned her. She was supposed to live free from the touch of a man, she had been promised that. While most would have cursed the fate that required them to live completely segregated from society and the opposite sex, the princess had no desire for either. As the Horseborn finished his ruthless search of her person, the princess still hoped something would save her from this man.

The Horseborn stood up straight as he finished. The headscarf was gone, forgotten in the recent struggle, and the Horseborn stood face to face with her more naked than any had ever seen the fabled warrior.

The princess stared at the face and realized that perhaps fate had not abandoned her.

"A woman," the Fortune Teller chuckled to herself. "That's the kind of surprise I've come to expect from the Horseborn … he's a woman."

She took the Prince's gold coins from the table and hid them along with all the coins he'd given her throughout the years. The copper coins he had given her as a boy. The silver coins he had given her as a young soldier. And, of course, all the gold coins he had generously given to the woman who always told him what he wanted to hear when he was a young general. It was good that she'd saved them, she would need them to survive. Her best customer most likely was not going to return. He would have to find another fortune teller to tell him what he wanted to hear. This was not going to end the way he wanted.

She walked back over to the table eventually. She regarded the spread for a moment and stood with her hand ready to scatter the cards. But for some reason, she stopped herself.

Maybe the Horseborn had one more surprise up her sleeve. And she was an old woman with little entertainment these days. She sat back down in her usual seat, placed her hand on top of the deck and closed her eyes.

The Prince had ridden hard through the city, to the outskirts, and finally to his prized princess' tower. He was not the only one who had made the short journey, however. The king had heard of the assault on his daughter's guards and had roused his own personal retinue and marched to the tower as quickly as he was able.

The two waited outside the tower for the Horseborn to bring the princess.

They did not have long to wait: soon enough the Horseborn came out of the tower escorting a figure robed in flowing silk from head to toe, the deep brown eyes being the only visible body part. The Horseborn led her to her horse first and helped the princess mount. She then led the horse straight to the Prince, ignoring the king.

"Give her to me," the Prince demanded. He fought to keep his composure and not grin.

The Horseborn looked up at the princess, then reached into the saddle bag and pulled out a large coin purse. "No," she said, holding the purse out for the Prince to take back.

"What?" the Prince again fought to keep his composure, except this time there was no grin.

The king, for his part, was not so skilled at keeping his composure. He openly grinned. "An honorable warrior indeed," he beamed. He offered his hand to help the princess dismount. "My beloved daughter," he made sure he said that loud enough for his guards and any nearby peasants to hear.

The effect would have been better if his beloved daughter has taken his offered hand.

The king's patience waned quickly. "Give me my daughter," he half-snarled at the Horseborn.

The Horseborn still held out the coin purse.

"Give her to me." The king then signaled for his guards to come closer.

"No," the princess said from on top the horse. "I won't be given again."

While the king stared at his daughter in shock, the Horseborn threw the coin purse down at the Prince's feet. Before anyone could stop her, she was astride the horse behind the princess with her curved sword drawn and ready. She waved the sword at the dead bodies strewn about the base of the tower. "I had no trouble with them," she said to the king's guards, "and I'll have none with you."

The guards stepped back.

The Horseborn kicked the horse and it galloped past the guards, past the king and past the Prince.

The king shouted at his guards to follow them. Most obeyed the order, but purposely took too long to ready and mount their horses so they would have no chance of catching up with them. The king was furious. He threatened his guards with imprisonment and death, and vowed to take his daughter back from the vile Easterner that dared steal her.

The Prince watched the king rant and rave, and quietly retrieved his coin purse. He would need to put it to good use if he was to salvage anything from this fiasco.

The Fortune Teller picked the top card off the deck, opened her eyes again and looked at the back of the card. She regarded it for moment.

Then she set it back, face down on the deck and with the other hand scattered the cards in the spread. It was time for the princess to make her own fate.

Undertow

Meredith Schwartz

Ella peered out from behind a column of alabaster. It went without saying that this ball was the most wonderful night she'd had since her father died. It was just that it was even more wonderful here, or between the rosebushes shaped like fantastical beasts, or in the little red-curtained alcove that overlooked the musicians. They were sweating so from the dozens of candles that the conductor had to keep wiping his cheek with a gold-braided sleeve.

Belle-mere and her daughters simpered past, and Ella fluttered her new fan in front of her face. Ella was in love with her fan. It hid her expression—by turns awed, giggling, and disgusted—and gave her something to do with her hands. Perhaps, if she asked very prettily, Godmother would let her keep it when the night was over.

She wasn't scared—she stamped her foot at the mere thought, and heard her slipper chime. It was just that she had no one to talk to. She didn't know anybody's name, or anybody's horse, or anybody's castle or daughter's husband's sister. But she had danced four dances with four different gentlemen and only tripped once. She had eaten handfuls of golden puffs, each with a surprise inside, and had drunk wine that disappeared like smoke on the tongue.

Only Ella kept peering at the footmen, no older than she, who handed round the food on heavy silver trays, and wondering what they were thinking. She said thank you to one, and some old biddy in a turban had stared like a fish before cleaning.

Ella had had to use the fan again. It was hard to remember all the things a princess was not supposed to see.

She looked at the prince instead. That should be safe enough. He looked handsome, of course—anyone would in blue velvet, with a great circlet of gold on his head—but he also looked gay and kind.

He was dancing with a girl in a shimmering green dress, and hair so pale it shone like moonlight. She had a solemn expression, as if she were minding her steps or her manners. Ella watched them until they were swallowed up by the swirling crowd, and felt a little hitch in her chest.

Ella shook out her skirts and lifted her chin, and determinedly marched over to the food again. She came face to beak with a giant ice swan in the center of a pile of melon unicorns, berry flowers, fruit that looked like anything but what it was. "I don't know what you're looking so smug for," she informed it. "They probably make their swans look like icicles."

A low chuckle came from close beside her and she whirled, startled, her wide hoop skirt lashing the stranger's legs.

Ella blushed. "I'm sorry, I'm not used to ..." she broke off. It was the prince, and he was offering her his arm. "Do you always talk to the food?" he asked.

"Pretty much," Ella answered. The food and the cats and the fire that was basically it for kitchen conversation.

The prince's eyes were gray, and the corners crinkled when he laughed. "What an unusual girl!" he said. "Come and dance with me."

Ella peered over her fan the way she'd seen Natalia practice in the mirror. "Is that a royal command?"

"Unless you'd rather have the swan."

By the time the musicians had struck up, they were both laughing so hard she had to pant for breath to dance. Between the whirling steps and the smoke wine, Ella couldn't see anything but a blur past the prince's face and his coin-bright hair. Maybe that was the secret. For a moment she thought she saw the green girl staring, but when she came around again, there was no one there at all.

Even years later, Ella couldn't remember what they talked about, she and Prince Charming, only that it felt very important. The bell tolling midnight caught her by surprise—surely she couldn't have been there half so long? But a smart girl doesn't argue with clocks or sorcery, so she dropped his hands and fled down between staring columns of dancers, pressing her hands to hot cheeks to hold back the stupid, childish tears.

It was almost a relief when the draped satin of her dress dwindled to tatters. The night air was cool on her skin. The fan furled to a single feather and blew away on the salt breeze. Mice chattered, and she lost a shoe kicking the pumpkin. There was a redolent thud of overripe fruit, and sweet juices ran in the gutter like wine. Good riddance to it, Ella thought. They were all right for red carpets, but against the cobblestones, glass slippers felt like walking on knives. It was almost a relief when the other shattered into shards. Ella walked on over them and kept going.

Ella's blood was dancing still, though the music spilling from open balcony windows had been replaced with the plash of waves and boats groaning at anchor in the docks.

She didn't want to face a scolding from Godmother for being late and insufficiently grateful or graceful. She wasn't ready to curl up by a hearth gone cold and patiently blow the coals alight again.

Ella hadn't meant to go down to the harbor. She'd simply run out of land, and she could still feel the tug pulling her onward. She wished she were young and foolish enough to believe she could walk out alone on the path the low moon cast on the water. She felt strong enough to walk right to the moon if it took all night, and never mind the sting of salt in the cuts on her feet.

But Ella wasn't sure she'd ever been that young. And she wasn't alone. The moon-haired girl was there before her, the one who'd danced with the prince, sitting on a rock and watching the tide go out. Her dress clung and twined round her ankles like seaweed. Her gown hadn't disappeared. It lay shimmering across her thighs and the wet black stone in a profusion of red gold green, changing with every tiny motion like the flash of a fish tail, something frightened by a child throwing stones into the pond and gone. Her hair whipped in the wind in tangled tresses. And she sat in the midst of this splendor as it if had nothing to do with her at all.

Maybe it didn't. The girl didn't sit like a princess, or a queen, or even a bourgeois baker's brat. She huddled on the rocky spur like a seal or a seagull or a street child, the kind that had no name. But Ella couldn't remember a time when a wild thing had not come to her hand.

She stepped closer, until she knew the other girl could feel the warmth on her back, and turned to see the source of her shelter from the wind.

"Hi," Ella said.

The girl looked at her for a long moment, and Ella wondered if she would run. But then she looked behind Ella to the trail of bloody footprints on the sand, and smiled.

Ella wondered if it was bad manners to look a gift mermaid in the mouth, but the girl didn't seem to mind. She stood obediently with her mouth open and her tongue stuck out, like a child in mischief who really had frozen that way, and didn't flinch even when Ella's chilled fingers pressed the pulse of her throat. Ella couldn't see anything wrong with it, except that no sound was coming out. It wasn't red or swollen, and it didn't have a big marble stuck in it or anything. Ella could feel the other girl's warm breath on her own lips as she peered.

She stepped back, a little reluctantly, and the other girl dropped to her knees again on the narrow band of sand, bordered by seaweed, that was still wet and smooth but no longer being swept clean by the diminishing waves. Little air bubbles pocked the surface, but she didn't seem to care.

The girl pointed once more back and forth between the fishtailed maiden and herself, and then started drawing something else with the sliver of shell like a waning moon that she'd drawn from her bodice on a narrow thong. Ella could see a little trickle of blood running down the curve of one breast where it had slipped.

This one was much harder, and Ella had never been much good at guessing games, even in the old days when she'd played in the parlor with visitors. She crouched down beside the girl to study it closer. An old woman with a knife, and a girl with what looked like little sticks or blades of grass underneath her feet. With the tip of the blade she pointed at the girl and herself and the girl again, and then drew an X through her throat.

Ella sighed. "Right, you have legs and you can't talk." The girl bit her lower lip, then reached over to touch Ella's bleeding feet, and then her own, which were smooth and unmarked, uncalloused even. Not too many rough roads at the bottom of the sea. Her fingertips were wet with blood and she smeared it across one elegant arch.

"It hurts … to walk," guessed Ella, and the girl smiled like it was the first time, like babies do, the smile growing with the sheer delight of being able to smile. Ella could feel her own face stretch in response and then they were both grinning like idiots, nodding at feet and stick figures and each other.

"But you were dancing with the prince," objected Ella, and then wished she couldn't talk either, because the smile was gone as if it had never been, and the girl was carving the sand in deep fierce strokes, a face Ella recognized before she'd sketched in more than the eyes and the curve of the mouth and the broad shoulders beneath them.

"Charming." The girl—Ella couldn't quite think of her as a mermaid when she was looking right at sturdy calves and delicate ankles—nodded without meeting her eyes and kept drawing. "Charming … on a boat?"

Another nod. Ella was starting to feel like each was a prize to be won. A familiar face appeared in the crude waves. "You saw Charming on a boat."

The girl nodded once more and pointed to the old woman and legs picture, and suddenly it all made sense to Ella. "You have a fairy godmother too!"

Ella sat down abruptly in the sand. "Mine gave me a dress—not this one—and a coach and a coachman and sent me off to the ball to meet Charming too. I think she expected him to dance with me once and propose marriage. Only he didn't, of course, 'cause he'd only known me for half an hour. Now she'll probably never speak to me again ..."

Ella broke off abruptly when she glanced at the other girl's face. "You're crying." She'd never seen anybody cry before without making any sound at all.

"Come here," she said, and then there was a big damp lump of mermaid in her lap, sniffling silently into her shoulder. Ella gave brief thanks that she wasn't still wearing the brocade, and then devoted herself to stroking that corn silk hair.

"It's okay," she mumbled awkwardly, "it'll be okay," because that's what Ella wanted to hear when she cried, even if it there was only Cook to say it any more and it was never true anyway. She couldn't remember what else her mama had said when she was unhappy, just the tone of her voice and heaviness of blankets sinking over her and the touch of cool white hands. So she began to sing instead.

It was only a silly little lullaby, something about many-colored ponies, but the girl stopped crying and looked up into her eyes with so much wonder and longing that the song caught in Ella's throat like a trapped bird. She touched her tears, and then Ella's throat, and then her lips, and Ella didn't know what she meant exactly, but she knew that no one whose weight was making your legs go to sleep should look so far away. So Ella kissed her.

She should taste of something besides salt and a hint of smoke, Ella thought. Something exotic, or at least fishy. But she didn't. Her lips were chapped from the sea wind and the white shoulders under her hands were warm and not as perfect as they'd looked from a distance.

"Look, you're getting a freckle," she said. The girl looked confused. Not a lot of sunlight under the sea, either, she guessed.

"I can't keep calling you 'the girl'," said Ella. "I'm Ella. What's your name?"

The girl shrugged. Right, thought Ella. How would you draw a name? It wasn't a thing you could touch like a boat, or a prince, or a mermaid with sunburn. Ella thought about giving her a new one—her mother's, or her own middle name that no one remembered. But it didn't feel right. You couldn't put your name on and off like a dress, even a magic one.

The girl traced her shell knife along the edges of Ella's lips. Ella wasn't sure if she was being silenced or threatened or drawn. The girl had to push her, gently, twice in the chest before she understood to lie back in the wet sand. Ella felt the flat of the blade slide slowly over the curve of her hip, the inside of a wrist, the back of her knee. A sweep of blond hair fell across Ella's skin from time to time and made her shiver, but she knew better than to turn her head to follow. She held very still and watched the clouds until she thought, if she moved, she might fall off the world into the turning sky.

The sand was cold and rough, the knife was cold and smooth, the stars were cold and white. It was a shock to remember the warmth of fingers, the wetness of mouths.

"That tickles," said Ella. "Tickles? Like this?" And then the two of them were rolling over and over, crushing out the pictures. The mermaid laughed without any sound. She had a strand of seaweed in her hair, so Ella had to kiss her again.

It turned out that gowns that shimmer have lots of little prickly bits that dig into the skin. Ella pointed out that there wasn't much left of her dress, so it was only fair that the girl take hers off too, and since the mermaid didn't answer, she considered she'd won the argument. The girl was getting goose pimples, though, her nipples tight and hard as though they'd puckered for a kiss. Ella decided it was only common courtesy to help her get warm.

They did things without names, then, which was only fitting. And the girl tasted like the sea after all.

After, Ella wanted to lie in a heap like the kitchen cats did when no one was looking, and tickle her mermaid with bits of her own long hair. But the girl disentangled herself and, still naked, crouched and began to draw pictures again.

Ella rolled over on her side to watch. The prince and the mermaid with a ring on her finger, the prince in his bed. The girl drove the knife deep into the chest of that picture, and glanced at Ella to make sure she understood, then drew herself with a tail again. Ella wondered what mermaids without thighs to part did instead of what they'd just done, but she didn't know how to ask.

The girl pulled her knife from the picture prince's heart and tossed it aside. She scratched at the sand, scrabbling with fingers like claws until she'd wiped it out.

"Hey," Ella said softly. "Hey, it's okay. It's just a picture. He's fine." She got up, then, and went to the girl to soothe her and pull her into her arms. But the girl threw off her hand with a fierce look and drew one last picture, of an empty sea, with waves. Ella thought the mermaid could just as well have taken the cuddle and pointed at the real sea which was right there, but she had sense enough to keep it to herself.

The girl pointed at herself, then at the obliterated picture, then at the waves. "If you don't have a tail you have to go back to the water?" No wait, that didn't make sense.

The girl looked frustrated. She crossed out the tail picture again. She tossed a handful of sand into the air. She pointed at herself, and the waves, at herself again, at the moon as it fell out of sight behind the edge of the ocean, and then finally at Ella's discarded rags and bare feet.

"Oh," Ella said. The girl was going to disappear, like her magic dress and her magic shoes and anything else beautiful Ella had ever loved. That appeared to be what magic was good for.

"I hate magic," said Ella. And then, in a smaller voice, "how long?"

The girl drew in a sun rising over the empty water.

Her mermaid came back to her then, and hung the knife around Ella's neck instead of her own. Ella knew what that meant. No more stories, no more talking. They sat nestled like spoons and looked out together at the tide coming in and the sky starting to glow like banked coals. The wind kept blowing strands of blond hair into Ella's mouth, and Ella wished she could swallow them whole.

Voce

Kimberly DeCina

Mama's tongue was like flint and her gaze was sharp as diamond, and no one ever argued with her. That was best, too, because when someone tried she'd run him ragged. Her eyes were swooping, piercing things that found faults and cracks in any armor, and her hands were rough and could hit hard when they did. She never struck me, but somehow I knew that. Everyone did.

Everyone came to our inn because the view was pretty, right on the border of the woods, though Mama sometimes wryly added that it "wasn't quite the view those ridiculous drunks meant." The brush crept right to the edges of our walls, and sometimes a befurred creature or two would lurk nearby, though never too close. Inside, there were tables to be served and food to be cooked, ale to be kept flowing so the customers stayed longer. The two of us didn't have much time for peace. And as we served a good full house most nights, we seemed to do the job well.

But Mama hadn't been the same since Papa died. Before that she'd smiled and even laughed now and then. She had danced at Christmas. She'd bought ribbons from the trader, who smiled and looked appreciatively as she tied her hair up and revealed the curve of her neck. Her face had still been set in hard lines, and her hands were red and rough, but she once had a bit of brightness to her that had faded since, something in her eyes that was a little kinder. But neither of us had cried much when he went. I'd never seen a tear from Mama, not even during the sickness or the night that he'd slipped away, and she'd barely given me two days of mourning before she said, "Amalia, I need your help now."

I didn't protest. There was an inn to manage and work to be done. Sometimes, though, I imagined him home and whole again, chatting with customers and swinging Mama around playfully when her frown got too deep. But this was something I never told her.

Mama worked hard and ran things well, and any red-faced offers to "run this place right" earned a man such a look he held his legs tight together in self-defense. If you told her she needed anyone, her face would get dark and her lip would twist a little. She would look at you, and the world would suddenly fall silent. It was then, without her saying a word, when you knew she could see every bad thing about you that ever was or would be. And you never, ever wanted to hear those things out loud.

I wanted those eyes. I saw them flare when she taught me, not the things other girls knew—how to pinch their cheeks to roses and dress to fit their curves—but old riddles and mindbenders, the way to carry five laden plates at once, how to step on a man's foot and make it look like an accident when he peered at you the wrong way. They were eyes that understood cleverness, knew about strength and bathed in them like they were moonbeams, far better than ever being pretty.

The trader came Thursday every week, like clockwork, though Mama hadn't bought very much from him in a long time. He had always stopped, for as long as I could remember, to bid us good afternoon and buy his lunch. I liked him; he had large brown eyes that seemed to smile even on the hottest or coolest day, he always tipped well, spoke softly, and he never drank. I also wasn't so young I couldn't see how he looked at Mama, the places where his eyes lingered and the extra care he took when he spoke to her—a subtle tilt of his head, an especially soft word. Whether or not she noticed, she seemed to treat him no differently. It wasn't until I was sixteen, though, that he brought his daughter.

She had been there suddenly, sitting on the end of his wagon one day, like he'd found her as a baby under a cabbage leaf and she'd sprung up overnight. My eye caught her at the window and it was held there, suddenly making me still. A few of my dirty plates nearly dashed to pieces on the floor as my body jolted.

No one my own age could have seemed more different to me. I had seen other children playing before, their feet beating out music on the cobblestones as they chased hoops and giggled in the sun. But she was fairer than any of them—both of hair, more golden than brown and plaited with a time and care I could never afford, and of face, smoothed into creamy skin and delicate cheekbones, an elegant nose. She was rounder than my stick-and-spindle limbs, and she wore her father's eyes well; they regarded the window, observing it simply and with no critique or guile. All this I noticed, knew, in a moment.

When she met my stare and smiled at me I felt ugly, when neither beauty nor plainness had ever mattered before. It took me two weeks to even speak to her, two more to pose the question of taking a walk with her. Her name was Catarine.

We would venture into the woods as if still young enough for expeditions, looking for trails through the brush and cutting our own if we found none. She was my guide, then, strange as that was and serene though she seemed.

Before Catarine I had never even tiptoed there, the world behind my home as uncharted and new as a blank page for us. But exploration was calling towards us, and she heard it beckon even when I didn't. She'd name all of the birds and the fluttering of insects, even when she didn't know the true names, fixing at least twenty different kinds of flowers in her hair before those days were through. She came closer to a squirrel than I ever thought possible, nearly nose-to-nose before it blinked and scampered away.

We found the best trees for climbing, as I bade her risk tearing her dress to find the hidden magic in knotholes and handholds. In branches high above the undergrowth we exchanged histories: her father's tales from town after town while her mother brought her up behind secure walls, the way a strange illness brought that life crumbling to ruin. From her mother's loss she knew the pangs of loss fresh and blood-flecked, not the scabs I'd patched on hastily, giving them two years to find purchase. And so she wept, when she spoke of it, and when she bent her head to my shoulder and clung to me I did, too.

She told me things beyond riddles and useful tavernkeeper's tricks, things no book would ever give credit to. What it meant when a cat sneezed, the story of the *querciola*, what to do against the evil eye—it filled my mind with a rush of the unknown, the quiet, tempting idea of mystery. Neither of us were children, in truth; we both had our monthly cycles, though I'd resigned myself to life as an old maid long ago. But she swore we had the hearts of innocents, that unicorns and winged sprites would fall at our feet if we only looked hard enough and believed. I looked and believed with all my heart, for her sake.

Catarine was a thing of lace and veils, just as much as she was made of leaves and twilight, and all of it so much lovelier than I. In time there was nowhere she went that I wouldn't have walked, no idea she could have proposed that I'd discount. My childhood came too late and went in the rush of a few months, all of them spent with her, traipsing home with my clothes covered in grit and my day wasted and idle. My mother's brow would arch disapprovingly when she met us at the door; I had never disobeyed her before, but for those brief days it never mattered. Something inside me was different, blossoming, always caught between a dance and a shiver.

"Child, tell your father I'd like to marry him as soon as he has the mind for it."

The proposal came unexpected, lightning-bolt quick, jostling my bones with its lack of romance and even further lack of necessity. The trader—Peitro on the rare days he spoke to me, perhaps Papa now if he accepted—had yet to see my mother raise her eyes to him, yet to earn anything but diamond, steel and flint, and yet there would be a wedding, and libations, and a sister. And all this less than a year after the man's wife had passed. I turned to meet Catarine's eyes, which were sunk low, her hands fingering something in her pocket.

"I will ask him," she said.

"Tell him," Mama insisted, voice carving the air, "that you will wash in milk and drink wine. And my own daughter will wash in water and drink water."

That proclamation—so strangely poetic, so totalitarian—had a hint of winter frost in it, and of more than idle promises. Somehow, I realized with a naked self-consciousness, I'd displeased her worth a heavy punishment. But I didn't know how.

Catarine nodded, squeezing her hand tight in her dress pocket, and turned around to walk out to the cart.

Later she would tell me—as her superstitions were his too, had been her mother's—that he poured water in a broken boot to see if it would hold all the way to the top. If it had spilled through, he would have refused, but the bottom stood firm. And so he accepted the next morning, bringing my mother a spray of wildflowers that she cooed over and promptly used to decorate some stranger's table. I would wonder, for a long time, why the fates had approved.

Catarine and I were put in separate beds, but she pushed them together the first night when I trembled beneath the covers at something I didn't know how to name. Her presence there warmed me, her hair curling against mine, and the long, smooth fingers of her hand twining with my own. I expected the shared space to be confining, setting nerves on edge. I had rarely been held before, even childhood phantoms earning just a voice at the door calling for a brave heart. And yet it was nothing of the kind, not with the way she fit against my back, the way her arms looped around my waist just so and made me strangely conscious of my own curves.

She murmured reassurances that night, voice tinkling bell-like against my ear. Wine dulled your senses, she said, and milk would curdle, more fit as a gift for the fae than for bathing, anyway. And my mother, for that was the subject that spun me up tight and made me pale—well, she saw what in its way was meant to be seen, a man with a wanderlust who needed safe haven for his daughter and healthy decisions made for their coin. She would talk, but talk was all it was.

"We are maidens," she told me, lips close to my cheek, the sound of her lulling the tarantella of my heartbeat. "For we are lovely and virtuous and so no harm shall come to us."

"You are lovely," I corrected her. My words spun out thin and flimsy in the dark. "I will be the hag of these woods before long, with you wed to a prince and guarded by your fae and horned horses."

"I desire no prince," Catarine murmured then, and there was a rustle, and a sigh, and then a thin circle of metal pressed into my palm. "Here."

I squinted in the dark as I brought it to my eyes, eager to make out its form.

"A metal button," she told me, and she spoke as somber as one talking of the saints. "A charm against *malocchio*. It came from my mother's dress. Keep it with you."

I stared at it helplessly a moment longer, feeling strangely heavy, before she guided our entwined hands to drop it in the pocket of my nightgown.

"Put it in your dress when you change in the morning, too. Have it beside you always. It will protect you, Amalia, shield you as I will. The evil eye won't have a single resentment for you."

And she kissed my forehead then, a soft and gentle thing that I felt long moments after.

"And this will protect you, too."

The water fell sharp and cold as daggers, raising goosepimples on my skin and making me beg for searing summer heat. But autumn was firmly inside our house, mercilessly chilly as I sat there and shivered, pouring icicles into my hair.

Not that Catarine fared much better, queen of some foreign land though she looked as she self-consciously stroked the cream down one arm, as if waiting for it to curdle. We exchanged looks over our respective tubs, trembling sympathetically, bearing this strange creation of our now-mutual mother together, never knowing its meaning.

At breakfast, Catarine only sipped her wine. And when I met Mama's gaze humbly, waiting for a look that would see right through me and shatter all protections, nothing was forthcoming. There was a hint of a curling of her lip, a flicker in her eyes that suggested more than I knew, something I knew better than to inquire out loud. For all her eyes could send messages, there was only one word I could hear in all this, one I wondered at.

Wait.

I clutched my hand tight in my dress pocket.

There was more to come and I saw it immediately. The next day there was a large tub of water for both of us. We curled as close together as if it were bedtime, hoping for a touch more warmth and comfort from each other's nearness. Trembling and numb I still felt her closeness, the awkward touch of hands and hips, her face close to mine but now reading blank as new parchment paper. I nearly touched her breast once, an accident I avoided at the last moment, pulling my hand back quickly to send ripples around us. I wondered, suddenly, if we were far too old to bathe together.

The third day, there was milk waiting for me, and water for her. That divide after the sudden, intimate unity, the metal edges of a too-small tub, the way water weakens milk—I felt it choking vice-like against me, with the sudden strength and clarity of a brick house not even hurricanes could move. It was as if I'd been played with, taunted with her presence and then thrown from her again.

And Mama smiled.

When one is not born an evil stepsister, but made, the change is by degrees. We were put to work together quickly, summers in the woods long over and now turned over to my teaching Catarine the best way to mop a floor, to serve a mug. I murmured tricks of the trade from the corner of my lips as we worked, for she was my sister—no, even more than my sister, and she deserved to keep step with me when we had thrust this upon her. But all this was in secret, hunting down cracks in the wall built between us and whispering into them when no one was watching.

A week of this and then Mama bid me rest, her smile genial enough to hide how it cut smooth and knifelike across her face. I accepted only reluctantly, glad to see her happy for once and fully intending to give Catarine her own respite in due time. But mother's work for Catarine stretched out longer and harder, the full load of it more than I'd ever dared take by myself. And my attempts to rise and help even a single task were met with a clucking tongue; the thought of defying it gave me pause. Something in me quaked at the thought that she'd look at me, pierce through my skin to find some secret, sleeping thing at my core and let her words brand me failure and monster.

My mother's pattern in those days was easy enough to guess, or so I thought: the luxuries and shelters I'd never before afforded, all gifted to me at my stepsister's expense, all caulking whatever cracks in the wall between us we'd managed to allow. As winter crept up on us I was given a coat of fur, while Catarine had nothing. The finest of our food and drink went to me, the closest place by the fire. Pietro, so often traveling the road to towns hunting for Christmas gifts, was able to see and say nothing.

I still curled up by night with her, murmuring my apologies, the position of our beds something Mama either had not seen or deemed unfit to be upset about. Her eyes regarded me slow and sad in those evenings, and I who was no stranger to hurt knew she felt it, saw it pool in her hair and the lines of her hands, the creases of her dress. I saw it in spite of sweet-voiced protests: "You have worked all your life, Amalia, and I've sat pampered and princess-like. Your mother sees justice in hard lines, but it's never faulty, it's not untrue—"

She was lying, though, not just mistaken or painting things brightly but spinning out a falsehood as sure as any sin for my own sake. And when she threw aside feelings of betrayal and kissed my cheek, murmured charms of protection, as if it were I who needed them, I felt wracked by guilt colder than any coat of fur could relieve me from.

It's envy, some will tell you, that creates a wicked stepsister. But it wasn't fully so for me. Catarine was beautiful, so much moreso than I, and even as hair turned limp and clothes grew threadbare she would be beautiful still. Lovely with reddened hands or covered in ash, graceful bent over dishes for hours at a time, but this was the beauty I'd always known, had walked and spoken and bonded with strong as a firmly-forged chain. And her kindness, for all I thought it far better than mine, was my balm and comfort too.

Covetousness, though, is envy's cousin. And this is what would stab through me one afternoon as I watched her work, saw the eyes of admiring drunks and envious wives who hungered for her youth. Watching her move among them, shining out of their midst, what made a wicked stepsister was the stray, stabbing thought that they couldn't have her. She was mine.

The thought was no innocent possessiveness of a childhood friend or clinging little sister, for she was my peer and we were far too old for such things. This was the culmination of half a year, of secrets whispered amidst the leaves and the weight of her arms in the evenings, her body glistening with water in the bath. This was Catarine at her most unavoidable, the way her too-innocent kisses burned, the way she was more than my sister, could never be just my sister, and calling her such would be a lie beyond any I'd ever dare tell.

Once such a thing is surfaced it can never be beaten down again. Some trace of it remained even in my most steadfast defiance, lining my thoughts with curses. When the evenings came and made my thoughts too weary for self-denial, it drew out of me like the cry of a trapped animal, desperate to be free and whole again.

She was a woman, and this bad enough, but now my sister too. Regardless of what means had positioned us this way, it was so. I felt a curious pain none should ever feel, felt myself soiled from the inside out with no way of reaching the growing stain. To have cursed and corrupted yourself in spite of every effort, there's a time that's eventually had where you know no sense. You only wish it burned away the way they burn witches and traitors, the way an oven can make meat safe for feasting.

And so, one day edging on Christmastime, I took Catarine's button from my pocket and threw it into the snow. And from then on no guilt could touch me, no remorse make me waver, and I bricked the wall between us as firm as obedience to Heaven.

In a few evenings, the beds were pushed apart for the first time.

My mother smiled.

This is what makes a wicked stepsister: to ache for beauty in all things but to know yourself ugly, to beg for a pure heart but feel yourself twisted and malformed from within. To reach out for a bit of grace, so forbidden to the likes of you that to preserve it and yourself you must hate it instead. I had known more than she ever did that I was not meant for fae and unicorns, anyway. I saw the darkness presented to me, knew that within it I wouldn't see her face, and so I leapt forward to drown in it.

December passed and stretched into January, then February, and I grew harder with the passing days just as the trees hardened with icicles and frost. Strangely enough, Catarine said nothing. Over time I wasn't sure what she would have thought of it if she even knew. The looks she gave me, though, were wounded and terrible, and I'd often wish I were blind and could avoid them.

The weather was fierce and hard, and seemed to leave Pietro stranded in town after town, even his letters unable to reach us. The man was good in his way, but I wondered if his eye hadn't roamed, instead. My mother's tasks, in turn, grew harder and more sadistic. Catarine was to wash the dishes within an hour and go supperless if she didn't, tend the fire when it hadn't had time to cool and nurse the burns on her own. Finally, Mama threw her a dress of paper and told her to go out and gather strawberries, eyes sparking and lip twisting dangerously as she commanded it.

"It's the middle of winter," I found myself saying, my voice falling insignificant as snowflakes. "There are no strawberries. She'll freeze—"

"Be silent, Amalia." And I was.

But Catarine wore the paper frock, which clung to her body flimsy as a cloud, and trembled underneath it. She took the basket, and a small crust of bread, and in a handful of minutes she'd met my eyes with a silent, shaking gaze and was gone. My stomach twisted in knots as I watched her leave. Mama meant for her to die, she must. For all my forced hatred in the world I hadn't anticipated that. And it was all I could do to not run out the door afterward, pull apart those defenses brick by brick. I cursed, even as I made my mind a blank slate, the fear and self-hatred that made me stay behind.

It was her return, though, that set the beginning and the end of things in motion.

Catarine returned three hours after she'd gone, her basket filled to the brim with perfect berries and her eyes sparking like tinder. She looked healthier than she had in months, the beginnings of lines fading from the corners of her eyes and her skin beginning to smooth itself back to fairness.

I emerged from my bed, where I'd curled up in the covers and tried to swallow down my worry, to meet her at the door. Mama stood there already, and for once her eyes were broken things, staring at the miracle before her.

"Good evening," Catarine said.

A gold piece flung itself from her lips, shining in the dim lamplight, and clattered to the floor.

The next hours were chaotic things, three voices bubbling up out of turn, sometimes at once, and clashing together trying to make sense of themselves. Mama hunted with frantic conviction for something to attack with—how dare she survive? How dare she find strawberries in winter, as if she were good enough for miracles?—as

Catarine stammered out the story, her cheeks pink with the cold and her exuberance, gold loose against the floorboards with each word. There were fairies in the woods, she said, little men who could grant wishes, who would reward kindness. They had taken her in and asked for some bread, and she gave it, and to help sweep the back step, and she'd done it. And they'd blessed her with this, with these coins, with a quickly renewing beauty. It was just like the stories told her, like her fallen mother had told her, and all that was required was a bit of kindness, and hard work, and—

By now there was a pile of gold at her feet, and it twinkled like a thousand tiny suns, mocking me. It was the wealth we'd never had, that Mama had most likely always craved. It was a magic that had never touched me, a childhood of stories and pretend play that not even my love for Catarine could return. It was the mother who had loved Catarine and let her believe, the patience and goodness I was too stubborn for, too angry, too twisted and sick inside to know.

I kicked out hard and scattered coins everywhere, aching so much I could barely speak.

"You're allowed to throw gold around like you're made of it, then?" I managed to choke out. "Wasteful girl! They've made you a freak, is what they've done!"

"Amalia, please." She shrunk back, eyes lowered to the gold-splattered floor. I hated that submissiveness, then, hated her for not defying Mama, or me, or telling me we could be together in some strange world of supernatural that would allow it. "I don't know why you hate me so—"

"They take your bread and demand your work, and *this* is a gift in return? No man will look at you without greed in his eyes! No one will think of you as *yourself* again!"

"Not even you?"

Someone had pulled the floor out from beneath me. I stood there, dizzied and dumb, trying to choke out some response. Mama made no move on my behalf, waiting patiently for it, but nothing was forthcoming.

"How do you think of me, then?" she added. "Your eyes match your mother's, the way nothing can move them, but they didn't always. Tell me, I—"

"That's enough." I'd never been so thankful for my mother's darker interventions, though I wasn't quick enough to stop her from striking Catarine with a force that seemed to rattle the coins piling up in the floorboards. My stepsister took a few frightened steps backwards, bowing her head again.

That was when I realized with slow, cold horror that they both knew. Perhaps they always had.

"Tomorrow," I managed to snap out, "I'm going to go pick strawberries." I rushed up to my room, careful not to trip on gold pieces as I went up.

The cottage was easy enough to find, when you're following the broken-branched trail of a freezing girl with you yourself covered comfortably in fur. It was certainly easy enough when I'd seen enough magic to know it existed. Through a watery-eyed blur I saw it, a ramshackle thing of twigs and stones, half-formed from the shifting crust of soil. I clutched my pail of bread and cake to me; Mama had insisted I bring it, as Catarine had brought her food, but none of it mattered to me ultimately. The last thing I wished for were more coins. I had other business.

They were good enough to answer when I knocked, three unearthly faces at the door. Three little men, just as she'd described: they were squat and brown, staring at me piggishly through small, round eyes and coarse beards. I glared back at them, a bit too harshly perhaps, for a long and awkward silence passed before one of them barked for me to come in.

I pushed through them to sit by the fire, their chair too small for my body, pushing me into hunched and twisted shaped as I struggled for comfort. "I have business," I muttered, as I studied the placement of me knees. "Business regarding a girl you received yesterday, a girl you worked magic over—"

"My brothers and I hunger," one interrupted, his voice like the shifting of soil across hours and years. "Have you anything to share with us?"

I didn't even touch my cake, the question making me bristle. "It's not polite to interrupt. And I've come through the harsh winter where hardly anything grows to see you, yet you beg my food from me. Earn your own."

Three sets of annoyed eyes met my defiance, but I didn't care. I was furious, at Mama's heartlessness and my own cowardice that so failed to stop it, at stupid fairy stories and their promises of air. My own dreams were impossible still, and why then should I give these false mystics any quarter?

"You worked magic," I began again, and as anger bubbled up fresh inside me I took the cake from my pail and tore into it in front of them. "You worked it over my stepsister, who now litters our floor with coins whenever she speaks."

"Your sister was kind and good to us," another gnome cracked angrily with the sound of ever-decaying leaves, "so we did reward her."

"*She* shared," muttered the first, licking his lips.

"You took advantage of a poor, lost girl fallen victim to cruelty," I snapped. "She believes in the triumph of her own self-sacrifice, and now she is robbed of her voice for fear of having to sweep up its remains!"

I devoured the cake messily, so quickly it was as if I were starving. I licked defiantly at some crumbs in the corner of my mouth, and started on the bread. Share your food, indeed!

"She'll receive a thousand proposals," my voice broke at this, "and none of them touched by anything but greed, she'll be seen as perfect, and pristine, and *freakish*—"

"There is a broom for you," the third one said, sounding of sleet and the frozen river. "Sweep away the snow at the back door."

"It was swept for you but yesterday and I am your guest, not your maid! Do it your damned selves!" My bread was finished and my stomach felt tight at the quickness of the meal. I flung the pail at them, eyes emblazed and hands curled into fists, my whole body tense and taut and raging. "You took her from me! You took her further than I can ever go, you touched her with something I'll never attain, and you smiled at it all and called it justice!"

"She was so much better off with you?" one of them cooed bitterly. My heart jolted and coiled in my chest and I didn't answer.

"She ran to the fae and begged them to embrace her." The sleet-voiced gnome gave me a look of long, somber ages, of sleepy decay. "There's many a road to escape. She chose one."

"If I thought I'd ever deserved it I'd have chosen it with her." It all felt too tight, too warm, too caged. I stood suddenly and rushed to the door.

"You wrap yourself in curses for the wrong reasons," one of them said, though who I could no longer tell, but I was already slamming the door behind me. Let them judge me as they would, but I'd thrown myself into the only choice I'd seen fit, and I'd done it so those scant months felt like ages ago.

I took trembling, pained steps into the snow, my eyes stinging against it, barely registering the door as it slammed behind me. I had fallen so low I felt there was no emerging, and I moved now with the conviction of a girl wallowing in self-pity.

I was halfway home when a rock twisted my ankle, pitching me forward towards the slush. Pain shot through my leg and I cried out, managing to catch myself on my hands but hissing as they began to blister with cold. My eyes stung with tears, as my breath began coming in tiny gasps and whimpers. Damn. Damn damn damn damn damn.

"Damn."

My stomach wrenched unexpectedly. I felt it writhing with the urge to vomit, bile twisting in its pit to heave cake and bread up through my throat and let me smell my own sick. It would have been fitting enough, perhaps. But as I gave in to the demand and let it squirm up my throat, thick and heavy there, it grew. It grew so that it made me panic, cough and heave wildly, all the while wondering if I would choke, and then it spat itself onto the ground.

A toad was suddenly squatting there, a wrinkled, ugly brown thing as low as I felt. It croaked once and hopped off, eager for a way to survive the winter.

So they had cursed me after all.

Still sprawled on my hands and knees, ankle throbbing, I laughed bitterly. In a handful of minutes they'd changed into sobs. I didn't dare form words, and a good half hour passed before I continued the travel home.

When I returned, Catarine wasn't home.

"I boiled yarn and threw it at her," my mother told me as I came in through the door, without so much as a hello. "Told her to go to the river and wash it clean. Perhaps this time she'll be so kind as to freeze. Did you find whatever nonsense you were looking for?"

"Yes," I said.

The wrenching feeling wasn't so horrible the second time. When the toad splattered against the floorboards I met my mother's eyes without another word and looked deep, seeing her with the clarity she had always seen me. I found the cracks and weaknesses there, the petty hatreds and unhealed wounds from mourning, the signs of how her heart had slowly frozen, her fear of what would occur if Pietro ever returned. And I liked to think that had she not been screaming at the creature on her floor she would have shuddered under my look. She certainly didn't frighten me any longer.

She was nothing compared to this.

I fled to my room and burrowed myself in the sheets, waiting for Catarine to return. But she didn't return that night, or the next night, or the next.

Mama spat out awkwardly that it was finished, then, and set me to work again. I wasn't permitted to speak to customers, and so the rumor circulated that I'd been struck mute, that the tragic loss of my stepsister had shocked me into the loss of my tongue. It might as well have been true. I was a thing in mourning, barely functioning from moment to moment, my spirit and my regrets with Catarine wherever she lay. As she'd grown more beautiful from her curse, mine seemed to lay me out ugly, thinning my hair and letting my eyes grow dull around my own grief. I began to be known as an unfortunate tragedy, a spinster in this place forever, to be certain.

When one is silent so often, she hears things. Gossip and tale tales creep around her ears, finding her far more easily than if she spoke. Tongues are as loose as if the world were drunk and, if they are drunk, looser yet. And so as weeks passed by and the year was firmly seated in March, hints of spring beginning to line the woods, a story began to piece itself together.

Had I heard of the girl who nearly froze to death washing yarn? What sort of silly fool would do that, in the dead of winter?

I barely paid it any mind, at first, didn't want to hear.

They say she'd nearly died, stupid girl, but a prince had been passing through. Princes in the middle of nowhere like this, could you imagine? Well, he'd seen that lovely young thing hard at work at her task, and fallen madly in love.

I desire no prince, I remembered her say.

And he'd swept her up right there, and rode off to be married. A princess born from love at first sight! Wasn't that something?

I'd nearly dropped a plate. Was there a chance she lived somewhere far away, lost to me forever?

That night Mama was already spinning schemes, half-mad things about disguises and switching bodies as

Catarine slept, tying the girl up and throwing her into the river. They were fancies, born out of facts we didn't know and chances we didn't have, and I was tired, so tired. My mind, muddied and fogged these last few weeks, was at least clear enough to know my answer, which came so crisp and ready it was as if it wasn't all my sixteen years in the making.

"No."

"No?!"

I knew her, for all she'd frightened me once, and I knew she couldn't stop me. "You spin your own webs and weave yourself up in them, and go mad trying to escape again. Enjoy it. I've finished. I'm an unnatural thing, perhaps, lower than these toads, but I'll bear that sin if it means that for a moment I may hurt less than this."

Mama had a tongue like flint and eyes like diamond and no one ever argued with her. But I was a thing of sharp edges too, borne up from loss and fear, the hate of my own needs, and still I knew I could never be one to cut people as she did. Of all the things to be in the world, to be her weapon was a choice I locked up then, in chains, rope and prayers.

Some coins still lurking in the floorboards, and a pail of cake and bread. It wasn't much, but it would do.

"You have nowhere to go."

"I'll manage."

I left her to sweep up the toads.

Had I heard of a girl offered marriage by a prince, but she'd escaped when they stopped to rest for the night only to die out in the cold?

… To find some great city and live there on her own?

… To vanish into the woods without a trace? Foolish girl, who would ever refuse a prince?

I'd heard many things, in fact, but the men in the woods would know the truth of them. It was where all my deepest instincts sent me.

As I left the inn behind, a flash of light against the snow made me squint and look harder. I pushed a hand through the clinging slush, ignoring the cold, revealing the details of what I'd spied. My legs rocked unsteady already against the force of my decision. The sight of what I'd found nearly made them give out again.

It was a small, round metal button, unmistakably Catarine's. It had survived the winter.

I picked it up with trembling hands, slipped it into the pocket of my coat, and set out again.

I knocked with an unsteady humbleness at the ramshackle cottage door, waiting for those three pairs of beady eyes and perhaps the further brunt of their curses. For the sight of her I would share the bread, though, I would sweep. I would live as their maid for threescore years if it meant seeing my stepsister again.

But it was one pair of large brown eyes at the door, and a small woman's hand brushing the knob, and a wordless noise passed between us, an astonished sob.

"Catarine."

A toad pushed through my lips, and crowded around her skirts. She smiled, a beautiful, broken smile, and scooped it up in her hand.

"Come in."

The fairies, I learned quickly, were gone. They'd left behind their fireplace, their chairs, their beds—"pushed all together it's larger than what we had," she pointed out shakily—but otherwise it was as if they'd never been there at all.

"Sews it all up neatly," I'd whispered, not daring to speak any louder. "As if we were mad and our afflictions … invented."

"Our need for the fae was finished." She'd touched my hand and I'd nearly jumped, but I'd allowed it, letting our fingers twine together as if nothing had ever seen that to its end.

"I've been a monster, Catarine."

"And trust will come slow and when it's deserved." Her voice shook for the first time that I could remember, and awkwardly she drew me closer. "But can't we just forget that for a moment? I've missed you so much."

I took her in then, fragile and silly and naïve, lazy when she wasn't pushed to work and self-sacrificing for the sake of longing to be pure. Submissive to a fault, maddeningly so, but damn it, she'd defied a prince and run. She was mine.

"You're my sister—" I began.

"Not by blood, and why do you think it's so at all? That your mother would swallow her pride for my father's modest earnings, far from a fortune, that she'd settle for a husband that's so far from home her neglect was too easy—what did she wish her grip on, Amalia, but you and me?"

"… we're making a mess of the floor."

Looking down at scattered amphibians and a treasure's chest worth of bullion, she laughed. Stroking a gentle finger across the spine of the toad in her hand, she smiled weakly. "Let's name this one? '*Malocchio*', I think. Did you know, toads sometimes bring the evil eye? And coins are a charm against it?"

My smile was a sad, hopeful thing. "Catarine—"

And then she was kissing me, and I couldn't think enough to say anything.

A girl who denies herself is a girl whose voice is poisoned, twisted, silenced. I learned this slowly, by degrees, as we mapped out life in that house together—which plants and creatures would prove edible, where the closest town could be reached. We promised to keep things meager, preferred it so, though we buried great caches of coins as treasure to be unearthed at a moment's notice.

Once we firmly seated ourselves in spring, we explored the land around us, and then, each other's bodies, the learning of each territory slow and patient, a building trust and a rediscovery of that which was already so familiar.

I wonder, sometimes, how deep our sin runs, if on some future day we'll burn for what we are. But as time passes and the toads grow smaller and infrequent, as Catarine whispers out pennies instead of fortunes, I know there's at least some force that sees how we fought against the magic that pushed us towards some other destiny, where stepsisters never love themselves and there is no mercy, where princesses are good and perfect and silent forever.

We've made a house of our own and forged our way, and soon our voices will be ours again, chiming out the strange and lovely resonance of life fought out together as both sisters and lovers will do.

Bird's Eye

Erzebet YellowBoy

The seas are parted by a vast continent that curves gracefully around the globe of the earth. The raven, from the clouds above, sees the foam of wavefall rippling over rocky beaches. The dark forest wraps about the high peaks that sprout up here and there. It appears as one great, emerald mass surrounded by diamonds, the sun tipping each wave with silver and gold.

As he falls from the sky the trees take shape. Scattered amongst the wooded depths, cerulean lakes appear like dabs of glistening color on a painter's dark palette. It continues, mile after mile, field after lake, peak after peak, from one edge to the other, across the wide land as the raven flies.

If he had the whim and traveled to the western edge of the land, he could view the crumbling tower there, now all but hidden by an overgrowth of moss and vines. It is very old; the mortar that held it together is mostly dust and the steps that led to its height now curl naked towards the sky. Once the raven frequented this place, but that was many years ago. He has since left the tower to the forest and his eyes alight on other things.

In days gone by there was a castle near this tower, and in this castle there lived a king, his queen and their infant daughter. Before the babe could even crawl the queen passed away from a winter's chill and the king remarried in haste to provide a mother for the girl. The new queen, however, showed no interest in the child, only in the wearing of the dead queen's clothes and her many jewels. The king was sorely disappointed but, being a kindly man, he did not chastise his new wife. Rather, he left her to her devices and spent all of his time caring for his daughter himself, teaching her to walk and read and write and ride while his queen aged alone. The princess grew into a beautiful young woman upon whom the king rested all of his hopes for the future of his kingdom; there would be no other children from the barren marriage to his second queen.

At last, the girl's thirteenth birthday approached. During the weeks beforehand the king prepared a great hunt in which he and his courtiers would kill the beast to be served at the celebration planned for his daughter. Many were the suitors to attend, each one hoping for the hand of the princess in marriage. The king would settle for nothing less than his daughter's happiness and had chosen the guests with care.

Into the queen's heart, however, a rotten seed had fallen, for though she whiled away the years in finery it had not been enough for her. The jewels and silks had never filled the hole in her heart, the hole in which this seed now sprouted and grew. Why should the girl be given any more than she herself had received?

There had been sightings of a fat boar in the nearby forest and the king determined that this boar would make the feast. Early in the morning on the day before his daughter's birthday the king set out with all excitement. On the eve his men returned to speak privately with the queen. The boar had become the hunter and the king lay dead, his blood on the ground and his body wrapped, unfit for viewing. The queen ordered the king's burial and all of the accompanying rites for two days hence, and then she smiled in such a manner as to scare her maids away.

The sun had not yet risen when the princess awoke on her birthday to find the queen sitting at the edge of her bed.

"The king has asked me to give his present to you before anyone arrives. You must hurry and come with me," she said to the sleepy-eyed princess.

The girl made haste, for she had been raised well and had no reason to disobey the queen, though her father's wife was still much a stranger to her. She threw her cloak about her shoulders and followed as the queen led her down the servants' stairway.

"Why are we going this way?" the princess asked.

"All is as your father has ordered," replied the queen. The princess said no more.

They soon reached the dark kitchen, where embers in the hearth sparkled warmly and the snores of sleeping maids mingled with the stirring of the cat. The queen and the princess passed out of the kitchen through a doorway that led to the herb garden. Into a hole in the garden wall they slipped, the queen shushing the princess whenever her foot fell too heavily.

The princess began to wonder at the glorious present it must be for the king to have set his wife about such secrecy. She could not imagine anything so great and was surprised when, after some time spent traipsing among the bushes and bracken that twisted through the wood, they came to the edge of a clearing in which stood a round tower that rose above the treetops like a mighty obelisk. Her neck ached to see the top of it.

"Is my gift this tower?" asked the princess, confused.

"No, silly girl, your gift is inside the tower," answered the queen, who then led her around to its far side where they found a small door mounted with a massive iron lock. In this lock the queen turned a key and the door opened with a mighty creak. It was a thick, oaken door, home to beetles and ants and all manner of creeping insect and the princess was afraid to pass through. Inside, she could barely see a stone stairway beginning its spiraling ascent into the darkness.

"Are you sure that my father has placed a gift for me here?"

"Your gift lies at the top of the tower," the queen responded, "and I am too old to climb the steps with you. You must go alone and retrieve it. There is a window at the top to light your way."

With that the princess began to climb the stone stairs, unable to see the queen behind her after the first turning of the spiral. The way was dim and she kept a slim hand to the wall even though she could feel the dust and the webs in the crevices beneath her fingers. The steps were broad and went up and up, around and around with no break in the walls encircling her.

"Queen, am I there yet?" she called.

"No, dear, you must keep climbing!" she heard the queen's voice returning from below. Upwards she went into the darkness of the tower, fear ringing in her ears.

She bowed her head and steadfastly, in her father's name, continued until at long last she came to another wooden door. It, too, had a thick iron lock on it, but was not fully closed. The princess pushed on the door and it opened onto a room lit by the rays of the morning sun coming in through one, oval window in the eastern portion of the rounded wall.

The room was opulent—as if out of a dream. A large couch draped with lush fabrics and a gilded dressing table upon which rested all manner of jars and bottles of scents and ointments graced the edges of the circular space. The walls were covered in tapestries of cobalt blue and the carpet on the floor was a garden of hexagonal florals. Rare and leather-bound books were strewn about on an assortment of tables and chairs. There was a small hearth, spanning an arm's length, in the northern wall and on the southern wall hung a mirror framed by silver birds, wings spread as if to carry one's reflection up to heaven. Upon a table lay a golden comb, the most fabulous comb the princess had ever seen. It was plain and worn with use, but it gave off a glow that warmed the princess' heart. Perhaps this was her father's gift.

The princess was enthralled, finding more things as she inspected each inch of the room. Garments could be found amongst the fabrics and by the couch several small chests held gems of all colors and shapes. The princess was so enraptured by the fine and shimmering vision before her that she did not hear the queen come to the door. Nor did she hear the latch fit tightly into its lock as she lay on the couch with her eyes closed, the golden comb held to her cheek. It was not long, however, before she grew hungry and arose to return to the castle to prepare for the events of the day. The door, she found, was closed tight, and no amount of pushing or pulling would cause it to open. She called for the queen, thinking that perhaps her voice would carry through the wooden door and down the stairway where the woman was surely waiting, but the queen did not respond.

It was then that the princess began to cry, wondering how it was she had come to be shut in this tower in the wood. What was she to do? She cried as the sun passed overhead and the room fell into darkness. It was shortly thereafter that she heard a scratching at the door. A slot at its bottom opened and a strange voice called out.

"Miss! Here's your dinner. I'll get the tray tomorrow when I bring your next meal." A hand pushed a platter containing meat, bread, fruit and cheese and a mug of fresh water into the room. The light from a candle briefly illuminated the meal.

The princess cried out, "Wait! Please! Can you tell me why I am here?"

The slot in the door was pulled abruptly shut and the princess heard the muffled sound of feet turning away. The tray of food sat somewhere in front of her, difficult to see in the weak light provided by the only window, now on the opposite side of the setting sun. She was so very hungry. She managed to sit by the tray and, very carefully, ate every last scrap on it. Exhausted from her calling and crying, frightened and alone, she curled onto the couch and fell fast asleep amongst the embroidered linens.

As soon as the tip of the sun reached the edge of her windowsill, the princess awoke. From her perspective on the couch she slowly allowed her eyes to travel again the breadth of the room. She filled the hours of daylight that her surroundings afforded her with coming to know the objects of her environment. Everything seemed to have been thrown about in a hurry; there was no order to any of it. Some of the clothing seemed old and frayed, the colors dulled by time.

The princess realized with a sudden sadness that these had been her mother's things. Whatever were they doing here? She sat at the window for a time with an old silken shawl in her lap, her fingers idly toying with the creases as she gazed out over the tops of the trees, seeing nothing from her vantage but the misted forest stretching out over the hills.

She thought to herself that surely her father had missed her and would, even now, be searching for her with his men. She clutched the golden comb in her hands all the day long, believing it to be the gift meant for her and the rest a terrible mistake. She did not know why the queen would have erred in such a way, but she calmed herself with the certainty of rescue by the king.

Shortly after the last of the sun's rays had faded from her window, she heard again the scratching at the door. Once more the slot was opened and a meal passed through.

"Wait!" called the princess. "Please! Can you tell me how I came to be here?"

"I'll get the tray tomorrow when I bring your next meal," said the voice behind the door, and then the slot was shut and the silence returned. As she had done the night before, the princess ate every morsel and curled up on the couch to wait for sleep.

It came to pass that the routine of her days and seasons established themselves and hope fell like the leaves of autumn as she grew to understand that no man would come for her, not even her father. When the first winter appeared, small bundles of wood had been delivered with her evening meal so that she could light a fire in her hearth and keep herself warm, and with the return of spring the bundles vanished. In this manner several years drifted by and the princess grew into a shapely young woman whose long, black hair puddled around her feet on the floor. Many hours of her time were occupied in the combing of her hair--one hundred slow strokes in the morning and one hundred strokes at night, the golden comb warming in her hand. She filled her days with reading, or staring out the window, sometimes talking aloud to the forest creatures that she imagined crept about her tower. The princess was very lonely, but all thoughts of what life she may have lived before had been put away and she no more called for someone, anyone, to come.

The princess watched as another autumn settled in throughout the hills and forest, turning the landscape into a wash of gold and red. One brisk day a large raven landed on the windowsill of the room. The princess had been sitting on her couch pulling her hair into a braid when the flap of wings drew her attention.

"Oh my," said the princess, blinking at the bird. "Who might you be?" she asked.

The raven was black as her room at midnight and his beady eyes the stars in the sky. His feathers shone with the sun gleaming blue and red on his back. His beak was as long as her littlest finger and his claws looked as though they could pierce through her flesh. He bobbed his head and chirped at the princess.

"If you come back after the sun has passed the window, I will save a treat for you," she said to the bird. He looked at her with an eye while the other peered out over the trees and then launched himself from her sill and flew off above the forest.

Later that day, after the sun had passed her window and the scratching at the door had come and gone, the raven landed again, his feathers silver now in the light of a round moon.

"I thought you'd return, for no one can pass up a treat," said the princess as she put a bit of lamb on the sill at his feet. The raven edged away from her hand, but as soon as she withdrew it he ate the bit of meat so quickly that if she had blinked her eyes, she would not have seen it happen.

"Hungry, are you?" The princess fed the raven a few remaining scraps and watched as he flew off with the last bite still in his beak.

"Do come back," she said.

That very night, curled into her small couch and covered in her quilts, the princess had a dream unlike any other. In her dream she was swept away until she saw a tower at the end of the world, fog billowing about its curving walls. All was dark but for one small spark of light that shone from a window at the top. Within that window stood a girl, her long hair spilling from her head in a sheet of gold that reminded the dreaming princess of her beloved comb, glowing in that same manner. Something stirred within the princess at this sight and she stretched her dreaming self towards the golden girl. In the window the girl turned and as her lively eyes met those of the princess she, too, reached out her hand. Just as their fingertips were about to touch, the princess stretched into wakefulness and the dream ended quickly behind her.

She rose that day with an unfamiliar longing in her breast and no amount of combing sufficed to ease her mood. The golden tool disturbed her, reminded her of the long, fine hair of the girl in her dream. Her day was spent restlessly pacing, the view of the forest below not enough to keep her still. When the scratching came at the door she hardly noticed the food on the tray until there, at the window, the raven appeared.

"Hello." She broke off a piece of fat and tender ham and put it on the sill. The raven stabbed fiercely at the meat with his beak.

"I had the oddest dream last night. Would you care to hear it?" The bird showed no sign of leaving as she added a bit of bread to the sill, thinking he might like some variety. He turned his eye towards her as she sat on a stool and told him of the strange girl in a tower so like her own.

"And her hair was the color of gold," she finished with a sigh.

So it went. The raven landed on her windowsill for his offering every night, preened and gurgled and then flapped away. Every night the princess dreamt of the strange girl in the tower so like her own, a tower at the end of the world, and every night she woke just before their fingers touched.

In time the princess became more familiar with the territory of her dream than of that outside her window. The season passed, the trees lost their leaves and the princess never noticed. Spring brought the rains and lush blooms and summer scorched it all away while the princess dreamt in her tower. The meals were delivered, the raven was fed and the princess slept, knowing nothing but her longing for the strange girl in her dreams which grew until the princess felt that she would burst, like an over-ripe peach, with her need.

The dream never changed, but the girl inside the tower did. With the passing of the seasons her golden sheen grew dull and her eyes lost the spark that first drew the princess in. Instead, they seemed like dim orbs that pierced the princess' skin with a need of their own. The princess stretched out her hand all the more, hoping to draw the girl out of her tower and into her own.

"O, raven, what can I do?" she spoke to his glowing eye one evening as they shared a meal.

The raven, in his wisdom, flew off.

That night the princess did not sleep. She could not face again the endless reaching, her open hand grasping the air, impotent. She sat on her couch, wrapped herself within the same silken shawl that once had occupied her fingers and began to comb her hair, one hundred strokes becoming one thousand. The hands pushed in the evening meal, the darkness deepened and still the golden comb moved up and down, smoothing her long black hair, one thousand strokes becoming ten. Daylight broke the night, the sun passed and still the princess ran the comb through her hair. For five days and four nights the princess sat in this manner on her couch, her hand never faltering, her hair gleaming as black as the raven's wing, her eyes open.

On the fifth night, the princess closed her eyes. Without the dream her longing had been much worse and so she let herself succumb to sleep where, once again, the dream unfolded. There before her rose the tower on the other side of the world and in the window the golden princess stood, her tresses flowing over the sill and into the darkness around her tower. The strands seemed to move as if alive, swirling in and out of the clouds, wrapping around the trees, until the longest strand reached across the world and snaked its way into the princess' hand. She saw then that the raven had carried the strands of gold in his beak. He landed on the sill and turned an eye to the princess and spoke.

"Princess, dark princess, let down your hair. I will follow the path and take you there."

The princess placed her golden comb gently onto the cushion beside her and stood, gracefully, as if hunger had never been. To the window she went, where the raven had been waiting, and climbed up onto the sill, her black hair falling to the forest below, flowing into the gold.

"Shall we go?" she smiled upon his feathery face. Arms outstretched as if to fly, the princess stepped from the ledge.

The night passed quietly and the sun soon rose, shining brightly into the window as the queen opened the door to the room in the tower. In secret she had delivered meals faithfully to the princess, wanting her to live and know the loneliness that had once engulfed her own meager life. When the trays had not been returned as usual, she had become suspicious and entered the tower herself.

She turned slowly and her gaze fell on rumpled linens and scattered books. Five trays of uneaten food drew flies just inside the door. The dead king's wife let the shock roll from her shoulders as she stepped over the threshold.

She walked the few paces to the couch, picked up the shawl that draped serenely over a cushion and held it to her face. Though the queen searched the entire room, of the princess she could find no trace. Stopping, she glanced at the window. There, on the sill, lay a single black feather, gleaming in the light.

The raven, in his wisdom, knew that no more treats would appear on the sill and so never flew that way again. If he ever had the whim to travel to the eastern end of that great continent, he could view the crumbling tower there. It, too, is very old and slowly sinking back into the earth from which it sprang. He already knows this place, for once he also landed there, but he has since left that tower to the forest and his eyes alight on other things.

Coyote Kate of Camden

Julia Talbot

"Well, I say we must do something! It has become an infestation. A plague, I vow," the Mayor of Camden, Colorado finished his oration with a stabbing finger motion that made his starched shirtfront flap up into his red face. He smoothed it down and hooked his thumbs into his suspenders, surveying the assembled citizens at the town meeting and pursing his lips. "What say you?" he added.

Virginia Harrow wanted to say that with his round face and bald head he looked like nothing so much as a colicky baby, but she hid that thought and her smile, one gloved hand rising to cover her mouth and turn her laugh into a cough. Even when the occasion was dire, as this one was, Mayor Brady amused her to no end.

"We've tried traps and poison, too," Chuck Weaver said, standing up, hat in his hands. Chuck ran the barbershop, which sat two doors down from Ginny's newspaper office. "But they just keep coming."

"They" were coyotes. Wily creatures, those dog-like coyotes, with their yellow eyes and their sly-smile muzzles. A whole passel of them had descended on Camden, swooping down on the outskirts of town and killing sheep, cattle and the occasional guard dog. Nothing the town had tried had even made a dent in the coyote population.

"Yeah." This from Nate Garrison, who owned the general store. "One of them even got into my stores out at the barn and ate half a month's provisions. What are we to do?"

Ginny had an idea, one that she'd hesitated to mention ere now, knowing it would be unpopular at best, jeered at in the worst. Still, Camden was in desperate straits. Why, just last night a large yellow mongrel had tried to steal the widow Freemont's daughter, right off their back porch.

She rose, smoothing her skirts and petticoats before clearing her throat. "Gentleman, if I may?"

Mayor Brady's face screwed up like he'd sucked on a pickle. "Yes *Miss* Harrow?"

Damn the man for insisting on emphasizing the Miss. He always did, reminding her of her spinster status. Indeed, of her bluestocking status.

"How about Coyote Kate?"

Silence descended for nearly a full minute. Then the entire assembly burst into shouting, some people protesting vehemently, some agreeing just as vociferously. Finally the mayor gained silence by pounding his gavel against the podium until wood chips flew.

"Coyote Kate," he said, spittle beading in the corner of his mouth. "Is a myth. She does not exist."

"That is entirely untrue, sir. Why, I have in my possession a letter from my newsprint counterpart in Lamar, Mister Edward Barrington, who swears by her services. He says that she may be contacted via his office. A telegram might even produce her help in a matter of two or three days."

"And how much does she charge for her services, Miss Harrow?" asked James McPeak, the town's only lawyer. "We are quite short in the city coffers."

Ginny gave him her best withering look. "I imagine, Mister McPeak, that our children are more important than a fat town bankroll. I, for one, would be willing to help pay the woman, should she actually provide a real service."

The noise level rose again, gradually, as people debated the merits of that, until one by one, farmers and rancher and miners all stood up to be counted as supporting Ginny's idea.

"I'll pay," hollered old Red Stines, his voice cracked from too many years of breathing hard rock dust.

"Me too," said Eamon Caskey, his Irish never so plain as when he shouted.

Finally so many people agreed that Mayor Brady was forced to take a vote. It passed in favor by a margin of three to one. Ginny would send that telegram tomorrow.

Coyote Kate was a colorful woman, to say the least. Ginny saw her arrive nearly three days later, riding in on a rawboned paint horse, little bells jingling on her saddle. Kate wore a long duster that seemed sewn together out of about five different dyed cowhides, the colors as diverse as the Colorado landscape that was her backdrop. Her hat sat as tall and high as any man's ten gallon, a giant feather waving from the band. Silver spurs on boots made from rattlesnake skin completed the ensemble.

With ink-stained hands, Ginny pushed her hair back and stood, untying her apron. No one seemed inclined to step out on the boardwalk along the street and greet the woman, so Ginny supposed it was up to her.

She stepped out of her office and into the bright afternoon sun. "Hello. I take it you must be Coyote Kate?"

"Yes, ma'am. I'd wager you're the newspaper lady. I hear you folks have got a coyote problem." Kate doffed her hat, revealing a person as bright as the clothing. Red hair, no doubt enhanced with henna, freckles and surprisingly wide blue eyes made Ginny think of a porcelain doll she'd once seen in Boston. The contrast between the face and the boots and spurs at the other end startled one, and stirred one as well, making Ginny shiver.

"We do," Ginny replied, her hand going to her own plain brown hair again, tucking it back into its knot.

"Well, don't just stand there, girl. Show me to whoever it is that makes the money decisions."

"Oh, I … well." She sighed. Mayor Brady would not like this woman at all. Of course, he didn't like women on general principles. "There will have to be a town meeting tonight. As most of the town is going to pool the money to pay you."

One dark brown eyebrow went up, and Ginny wondered if that was the natural color of Kate's hair. Kate just stared at her a moment before shrugging and laughing, the sound gut-deep and infectious.

"Uh huh. How about showing me to the saloon, then, dearie?"

"Of course. It's just down at the end of the street there, and one block off." Ginny pointed to the west end of town. She'd never been in the saloon. Women did not indulge. She should have known Coyote Kate would.

Her very dear friend and fellow news writer, Edward Barrington, had sent a reply to her telegram, affirming that Kate would come. "She is unorthodox," he had said. "Quite unlike anyone else in my experience. Have a care."

Kate was quite unlike anyone in Ginny had ever met as well.

"No, no, honey. You need to come with me. I'm here due to you, after all. Least you can do is have a drink with me."

"I don't drink," Ginny blurted, her cheeks hot.

"That's a shame. You can have a sarsaparilla." Kate grabbed her elbow, and before Ginny could blink they'd gone halfway down the street, Kate's spurs clinking and Ginny's skirts catching on them.

So shocked was she by the sudden change of events, Ginny managed not a word or deed until the arrived outside the door of the *Dog and Pony*. Then she dug the heels of her very sensible lace-up shoes into the ground. "I think not, Miss Kate."

"Just Kate, if you please." She got an arch look. "You being un-neighborly? 'Cause I might be made to feel unwelcome and leave town."

"No!" That would never do. The town fathers would have her head, as once they'd agreed to have Kate come they had decided it was their idea. "I'll have a drink with you."

Kate smiled, looking for all the world like a babe in the woods. Or a sheep in wolf's clothing. She nodded, red locks bouncing, shining in the sun. "Good. Oh, honey. What fun we're gonna have until nightfall."

Ginny sat very quietly at the town meeting. Really, whiskey had an extraordinary affect on her. How could she have known, though? So instead of opening her mouth and telling Mayor Brady that he looked like a squalling infant, or worse, bursting into uncontrollable giggles, she folded her hands in her lap, kept her eyes straight ahead, and listened to Coyote Kate haggle.

"Now, sir, really. You know very well that twenty-five dollars is a paltry sum for my services."

"Madam, I assure you, we cannot pay you more." Brady blustered, his face going from bright pink to dark scarlet.

A giggle escaped, and Ginny clapped her hand over her mouth, drawing a few censorious looks.

"Well, then I'll just take my things and go. Good night to you, sir. Good night to you all."

Wide-eyed, Ginny stared at the Mayor, then looked around at her friends and neighbors. Surely they wouldn't let Kate leave. In the three days since Ginny had sent the telegram, two more sheep had died, and another child had been scared nearly to death.

Indeed, it looked as though the men of the community were more than ready to let Kate waltz right out the door. Ginny stood, her chair clattering back, ready to denounce the whole company. It proved unnecessary as the door flew open and the widow Freemont burst in, nearly in hysterics.

"My daughter! My daughter is gone. Oh, Mayor Brady you must do something. Those foul creatures have taken my daughter."

Appalled murmurs sprang up all around, rising to a roar. The townsfolk could finally all agree on something ...

"Pay her the fifty dollars, damn you."

"We'll pay!"

"This has to stop."

Looking as though he might succumb to an apoplexy, Mayor Brady stepped forward, spreading his hands. "Very well, Coyote Kate," he said. "Fifty dollars."

Smiling, Kate stuck out her hand. "Sounds fine, pardner. Just fine. Oh, and one other thing."

Brady hesitated, hand halfway out to meet Kate's. "What?" he asked.

"I want one of your young women. Don't care much which. I need to start training an apprentice. The only thing I'm a stickler on is that she has to be a virgin."

Brady actually took a step back. "I beg your pardon!"

"You heard me, you toady little man. That and the fifty, or I leave."

"Please." The widow Freemont touched Brady's arm. Her tears flowed freely. "Please."

A sly look crept into Brady's piggy eyes. "Very well, madam. If you retrieve the widow Freemont's daughter, alive and intact, and rid us of our coyote infestation permanently, you will have your money, and your apprentice."

Ginny's heart fell, and sobriety settled over her. She could see no way in which Kate could retrieve little Annie Freemont now. Mayor Brady was about to welsh on a deal.

Coyote Kate, however, only nodded, bells and spurs jangling as she shook Brady's hand at last. "You got yourself a deal, mister," she said. "And a deal's a deal."

The whole town waited with bated breath to see what Kate might do. Seemed she waited long enough, not making her move until well after Ginny's tiny wall clock struck midnight. The only reason Ginny knew anything of it at all was that she could not sleep, for the moon sat high and bright in the sky, and the coyotes were howling like a chorus of demons straight from hell.

Since Kate's horse still stood outside her door, Ginny heard it when Kate came out and mounted up. A quick glance out her window showed the fine figure of a woman in full regalia, hat in place, duster flowing over the horse's rump. Kate held something in her hands, something that resolved itself into a fiddle and bow, causing Ginny to wonder. She pressed her face to the thick glass of her small upstairs window and watched, and listened, as Coyote Kate began to play.

Sweet and mournful, the fiddle music filled the night. Kate's playing astonishing Ginny with its skill. She actually swayed along to the lament, humming it under her breath. She knew it … what was it?

As she watched, Kate spurred her mount down the street, toward the edge of town, and to Ginny's everlasting astonishment, dark shapes began to slip out of alleys and from under porches, tails waving like flags as the coyotes followed Kate right out into the night, out where civilization ended and the plains began. By the time Kate rode out of sight, her fiddle no longer audible, she must have had two hundred animals trailing her, howling an eerie counterpoint to her melody.

Ginny had never seen anything like it in her life.

Lighting a lamp, she scurried down the stairs, each narrow riser creaking under her bare feet, her nightgown and shawl flapping around her. She must record the whole event for the newspaper, else she think she'd only dreamed it.

No one would believe what Coyote Kate could do.

Not unless she told them.

Ginny woke the following morning with the sun shining on her bent head, her hand quite asleep where it sat, propping up her head. At least she hadn't drooled. Her eyes felt as though a dust devil had come through them in the night, but when she looked at her work table, Ginny was pleased as punch to see she had finished laying out her story. Only inking and printing remained.

She did go above her shop to wash up and dress first, and by the time she got back down, Johnny Alberts waited for her, his straw colored hair standing up wildly, a huge smile on his teenaged face.

"Miss Harrow! You got to come. Coyote Kate done brought Annie Freemont back, all in one piece-like."

"You've got to," she corrected automatically. "Has she indeed? How extraordinary."

Grabbing up her sketchbook and a nub of pencil, Ginny pelted after Johnny as he ran toward the town meeting house. She tripped on her bothersome skirts, but made it there just in time to hear Kate's ringing voice proclaim her success.

"All righty, Mayor. I brought back your girl, and the coyotes are gone. Pay up."

"Now, Miss Kate, how do we know they're gone for good?" Mayor Brady ran a finger around his starched collar.

"Because I run 'em off a cliff into the river, that's how. They're all drowned. Pay up."

"Nonsense! We have no way of knowing the truth of your statement." Oh, Brady just dug deeper and deeper into his hole.

Kate's face darkened to the point where her freckles blended right in with her flush. She stabbed a finger at Mayor Brady's chest. "Fine, then. Don't pay me. You'll see I don't lie. I'll be camped just outside of town. When you're ready to pay, just send the girl you promised on out with the money."

Whirling, multi-colored duster swirling around her, Kate headed for the door. Her spurs not so much jingling now as clunking.

Ginny cast a pleading look at the mayor, the sheriff, anyone who might do what they had promised. Chills ran down her spine and goose bumps rose on her arms. She couldn't help thinking they'd made a very big mistake. So big in fact that she turned, and, lifting her skirts to achieve an undignified trot, followed Kate out the door.

"Miss Kate! Please. Wait."

Turning, Kate put her hands on her hips, looming over her, a more imposing presence now than she had been the first day. The thunderous frown Kate turned upon her helped not at all. "What do you want, honey."

Grasping her courage with both hands, Ginny took a deep breath and made her offer. "I have some money … I put it aside. I could pay you."

"Oh, honey," Kate said, flinty eyes softening. "It's not your job. Those rotten sons of bitches need to pay their debts is all. Don't you worry. I'll get what's mine."

"But I really think—"

"Can you give me a virgin, honey?"

She looked down at her hands, her cheeks flaming. "I … well. No."

Kate hooted, clapping her on the shoulder. "Well, there you go. Thanks for trying, honey. Close your window at night."

"My windows?" She glanced up at her rooms above the shop. "Why?"

Kate grinned, hopping up on her horse and spurring around toward the end of town she'd come in from. "Just do it, honey. My little gift to you for being an honest woman."

Then Kate was gone, riding off into the midday sun, the very sight of it hurting Ginny's eyes. What on earth had they done?

In the days that followed the town woke each morning to a hysterical mother, proclaiming her daughter missing. One morning it was Lila Chen, the launderer's wife. The next it was Delia Clemens, crying into her fine linen hanky, her hair mussed for the first time in Ginny's acquaintance with her. By the third day it was Mayor Brady's niece gone missing; his sister's wails could be heard from one end of town to another.

The situation produced yet another town meeting. Really, they'd had more in the last month than they'd had in three years.

"We need to form a posse and go after them!"

"No, we need to pay Coyote Kate."

"Are you crazy?"

The voices rose in cacophony, causing Ginny to clap her hands over her ears, so that she missed Mayor Brady talking to her until he tapped her shoulder.

Ginny blinked. "Yes, sir?"

"You brought her here," he said. "You get her to stop."

Righteous indignation rose in her chest and she stood, poking at him, her finger sinking in just above his gut. "I tried." She poked. He backed up a step. "You wouldn't pay her. You reneged. I tried to give her money before she left town and she wouldn't take it. She warned you. And she's not a liar. Have you seen even a single coyote?"

"No. But something is stealing our young women. Our …"

"Virgins?" she asked, her eyebrows rising. "Well, you have only yourself to blame."

"Please, Miss Harrow." It was Lila Chen, coming to put one delicate, bleach bluing chapped hand on her sleeve, dark eyes full of tears. "Please help get my daughter back."

She could resist any and all of the men, but how could she resist a woman who had lost her daughter? Hadn't she called in Coyote Kate just to save the children of Camden? All of the girls who'd been taken were old enough to go on their own accord, but still too young to know better.

Ginny sighed. "I'll do what I can."

Ginny went to bed with her window open that night.

The sound of fiddle music woke her, sometime in the middle of the night. Sweet, not mournful, it came in on the breeze, the moonlight seeming to dance to its tune. Time to go.

She was already dressed in her split skirt and shirtwaist, all Ginny had to do was assume her boots and coat before heading out into the night, following the strains of the waltz that floated to her from just outside town. Right where Coyote Kate said she'd be camping.

A small light appeared as she rode closer, glowing, probably Kate's campfire. Sure enough as Ginny dismounted at Kate's camp, ground tying her pony, the warmth and light of it drew her, almost as much as the music that trailed off as soon as she stepped into its glow.

Kate sat on a flat rock, fiddle under her chin, the bow still set against the strings. "Well, they sent you did they, honey?"

"They did." She dug in her coat pocket. "The mayor sends his compliments."

Carefully setting the fiddle aside in its case, Kate rose and took the money, her fingers touching Ginny's causing a strange tingling under Ginny's skin. "Thanks, then."

"Where are the girls?"

"Safe. Back in the canyon yonder." Kate smiled, and she looked so different without the coat and boots and all of the other trappings that Ginny just stared.

Really, the woman was beautifully put together. So unlike her, Ginny thought, to notice such things, to see the curve of a woman's hip or breast and blush. "Have you enchanted me like you did them?"

"Oh, I don't know, honey. The spell is only supposed to work on virgins, but I'm beginning to think you don't have any in Camden."

"You mean Amelia Clemens? She's not?" Goodness.

"None of them are."

Ginny drifted closer, fascinated with the woman in spite of herself. "Why do they need to be virgins?"

Kate stepped closer, hand closing on her arm, callused fingers rubbing as they clasped Ginny's wrist. "Why do you want to know, honey? Are you actually one?"

"I … perhaps."

"I want a virgin so I can have a girl who has never felt a man's touch." Closer and closer Kate came, until finally Ginny could see each individual eyelash, each little freckle on Kate's cheeks. "So I can do this …"

Kate kissed her. Just put her mouth right against Ginny's and pressed down, opening her lips. Ginny gasped, letting Kate in, feeling the dampness of Kate's tongue on her lower lip, then inside. Her whole body trembled with the shock of it, sensation zinging from her breasts to her privates. When the kiss ended all she could do was nod.

"I can see why you'd want to be the first to do that..." she said, feeling dazed, realizing only when she tried to move that her hands were buried in Kate's bright hair.

"Am I the first with you?"

Ginny nodded. "You are. I told the Mayor he would keep his word if it killed him. It may have. He was terribly angry."

"He'll live," Kate said. "You staying with me?"

"Yes. I said I would." The prospect had terrified her before. Now Ginny found it pleasing. "And you'll let the girls go and leave Camden?"

"I'm a woman of my word. I'll do what I promised."

"Then I'll come with you and be glad." They were both honest women. Sometimes that was all it took to rid a town like Camden of its worst nightmare. Ginny wondered where Coyote Kate would be called next.

She couldn't wait to find out.

The Authors

Kori Aguirre-Amador is the author of several books including *Writers Anonymous* and *The Demigod Squad.* She lives in Draper, Utah.

Kim DeCina is 23 years old and lives in South Florida. Though she has been writing since elementary school, this is her first published full-length story. She is also the co-author of the paper "Of Dementors, Dark Lords, and Depression," a DSM-IV-style look into the psychology of the Harry Potter universe. Kim loves fairy tales in all forms, especially re-imagining them, seeing what makes them tick, and how they relate to reality more than we think. She is fond of both coins and amphibians.

Frank Fradella is the author of more than a dozen books, including *Valley of Shadows* (Cove Press), *Swan Song* (New Babel Books) and *The Complete Idiot's Guide to Drawing Basics* (Alpha). As a video producer he has done work for TurnHere, the Yellow Pages, Simon & Schuster and was hand-picked to produce segments for NBC's new travel site.

Frank is an independent filmmaker in pre-production on his first feature-length movie, *Fu & Far Between*, and was the creative force behind the award-winning magazine, *Cyber Age Adventures*. He is the creator of two popular tarot decks, including the world's first complete superhero tarot deck. He has been studying Chinese for several years and lives in Beijing.

Most recently, Frank became the host of the Beginner series of lessons over at http://ChineseClass101, putting his first-hand experience of living in China to work for those who are new to the language. He can be found online at www.frankfradella.com.

AJ Grant has been writing for over thirty years, provided you count the early years of crayon scribbles to be great writing, which AJ's parents do, thank you very kindly for asking them.

In addition to fridge doors, AJ's work has appeared in Salon.com, About.com, Torquere Press, Reflection's Edge, local newspapers, and even MTV (though the less said about AJ and that snake the better).

When not obsessively typing away at the keyboard, AJ cooks, gardens, reads, knits, worships at the alter of TiVo, is dominated by two cats, and twitches like an addict until the keyboard is once more in hand again.

R. Holsen lives in Asheville with a laconic partner and a pair of very communicative cats. Her interest in history and anthropology stems from an overabundance of folklore as a child, though her interest in telling stories cannot be so easily attributed. Currently she works in the family business peddling supplies to the artists and crafters of the Appalachians and beyond, though she holds out hope for becoming a published novelist and author of urban fantasy and mystery, with world famous to follow thereafter. To that end, she has published three short stories thus far; the third is reprinted in this edition.

Meredith Schwarz is the editor of Alleys and Doorways, an anthology of LGBT urban fantasy also originally released from Torquere Press in 2007. It is scheduled to be reprinted by Lethe Books in 2009.

Julia Talbot has been assimilated by Texas, where there is hot and cold running rodeo, cowboys, and smoked brisket. A full time author, Julia has been published by Torquere Press, Suspect Thoughts, Pretty Things Press, and Changeling Press. She can most often be found in coffee shops and restaurants, scribbling in her notebook and entertaining other diners with her mutterings.

Born in the Pacific Northwest in 1979, **Catherynne M. Valente** is the author of *Palimpsest* and the *Orphan's Tales* series, as well as *The Labyrinth, Yume no Hon: The Book of Dreams, The Grass-Cutting Sword*, and five books of poetry. She is the winner of the Tiptree Award, the Mythopoeic Award, the Rhysling Award, and the Million Writers Award. She has been nominated nine times for the Pushcart Prize, shortlisted for the Spectrum Award was a World Fantasy Award finalist in 2007. She currently lives on an island off the coast of Maine with her partner and two dogs.

Regan Wann lives in rural Kentucky with her husband and scads of rescue animals. She is currently completing her Master's Degree in English Literature by writing her thesis on the persistence of the fairy tale princess as a cultural icon. In 2008 she opened a small tea shop called Through the Looking Glass in Shelbyville, KY and would love it if you came to see her there. She is gratified, honored, and pleased to be a part of this collection.

Erzebet YellowBoy is the editor of *Cabinet des Fées*, a journal of fairy tale fiction, and the founder of Papaveria Press, a private press specializing in handbound limited editions of mythic poetry and prose. Her stories and poems have appeared in *Fantasy Magazine, Jabberwocky, Goblin Fruit, Mythic Delirium, Electric Velocipede* and others and her second novel, *Sleeping Helena*, is appearing in 2010. Visit her website at www.erzebet.com for more.

About the Editor

JoSelle Vanderhooft is the critically acclaimed author of poetry collections *The Minotaur's Last Letter To His Mother* (Ash Phoenix, to be released by Sam's Dot Publishing in 2009 or 2010), the 2008 Stoker Award-nominated *Ossuary* (Sam's Dot Publishing), *Desert Songs* (Cross-Cultural Communications, forthcoming), *The Handless Maiden and Other Tales Twice Told* (Sam's Dot Publishing, 2008), *Fathers, Daughters, Ghosts & Monsters* (VanZeno Press, 2009), *The Memory Palace* (Norilana Books, 2009) and *Death Masks* (Papaveria Press, 2009), the novels *The Tale Of The Miller's Daughter* (Papaveria Press) and *Owl Skin* (Papaveria Press, forthcoming) and *Ugly Things*, a collection of short stories from Drollerie Press to be released in 2009. She is currently at work on a series of novels for Drollerie Press as well.

Her poetry and fiction has appeared online and in print in a number of publications, including *Cabinet des Fees, Star*Line, Mythic Delirium, MYTHIC, Jabberwocky, Helix, The Seventh Quarry* and several others. An assistant editor of a gay and lesbian newspaper by day, she lives in Salt Lake City, Utah with her family and four cats.

CPSIA information can be obtained at www.ICGtesting.com
Printed in the USA
LVOW042111020712

288576LV00001B/45/P

9 781590 212233